MYSTICAL FORCE

CRAIG WEIDHUNER

Mystical Force Volume 3: The Kolri and the Koldar
Copyright © 2021 by Craig Weidhuner
www.authorcraigweidhuner.com

All rights reserved. No part of this publication
may be reproduced, distributed, or transmitted
in any form or by any means, including
photocopying, recording, or other electronic
or mechanical methods, without the prior
written permission of the author, except
in the case of brief quotations embodied
in critical reviews and certain other non-
commercial uses permitted by copyright law.

Tellwell Talent
www.tellwell.ca

ISBN
978-0-2288-5877-5 (Hardcover)
978-0-2288-5878-2 (Paperback)
978-0-2288-5876-8 (eBook)

Volume 3:
The Kolri and the Koldar

8

LOCATION: A SMALL MOM AND POP SHOP, TEIKOKU CITY

The Poison Starfish gang was one of the most notorious crime syndicates in all of Teikoku City. Their leader was a man named Kojiyama. On the surface, he appeared to be a simple businessman who ran a shipping and logistics company. However, this was a cover for his criminal operations. People from within and outside of Oyashima came to him to smuggle various illegal merchandise in and out of the country. Yet this was still only part of his criminal empire. Kojiyama had his hands in everything. From drug trafficking to counterfeiting, to illegal gambling rings, even racketeering, and extortion. This was the case tonight. A small group of thugs was visiting a small shop located in an unassuming suburban neighbourhood of Teikoku City. For an exorbitant fee, the gang members would offer "protection services" to small businesses. To help ensure that nothing bad would happen to them. Those who couldn't pay would often find themselves the victims of "unfortunate accidents." This was why five thugs were visiting this small convenience store. The owner had fallen behind on his "payments," so the Poison Starfish had gone to collect.

"Please," the shopkeeper begged, "it's all I have!"

The leader of this group of thugs took the box with the money. "This ain't enough. We already told ya, if ya want the protection of the Poison Starfish gang, ya gotta pay up. Otherwise, we can't protect you if ya were to have an 'accident'!" The leader of this group took an item off the shelf and dropped it on the floor, smashing it, "Oops, an accident," he said, his tone dripping with sarcasm.

"I don't have anymore!" the shopkeeper tried to explain, "Please, you've already come three times this week to rob me!"

"We ain't robbin' ya; we're here to collect 'payment' for our 'protection services,'" the leader explained.

"Forgive me," a female voice called out from the shop entrance, "I'm new to this planet, and there's much about your culture I still don't understand, but doesn't the customer typically have a choice as to whether they *want* your 'protection services' or not? I mean, it doesn't seem fair to expect people to pay for services they didn't ask for."

The Poison Starfish turned to face the voice. Standing right behind them was Shi-ria. "It's you!" one of them pointed at her. He recognized her from the description his gang members provided. Three months ago, the Poison Starfish had been hired to smuggle ancient artifacts into the country when Shi-ria suddenly showed up in the middle of the sale. Kojiyama told all of them to keep an eye out for Shi-ria. Assuming she was responsible for everything that happened, he ordered the Poison Starfish to make her pay for what she had done. "You're the one the boss told us about! The one who ruined the sale at the harbour!"

"That was an accident," Shi-ria told them.

"Well, you're about to have another 'accident'!" The leader of the Poison Starfish drew a small knife and lunged at her.

Shi-ria simply grabbed his arm and twisted it until the pain forced him to drop the knife. "Oops, another accident," she said mockingly, throwing his own words back at him. Shoving him away, another hoodlum came at her, fists swinging. Shi-ria effortlessly blocked all his blows. Grabbing his arm, she twisted it behind his back, then her free hand delivered a chop to the back of his head, causing him to fall flat on the ground. And so, each one of the Poison Starfish went after her, and Shi-ria took down each one with little effort, mocking them with their own words, "Oh my, another 'accident'! And another! You guys sure are clumsy!" When it was all over, the Poison Starfish lay sprawled on the ground, gasping and groaning in pain. Shi-ria stood over them, shaking her head, "You boys should learn to be more careful. Maybe then you wouldn't have so many 'accidents'!"

Walking over to the leader of the Poison Starfish, Shi-ria bent down and picked up the box with the shopkeeper's money. She walked over to the shopkeeper and handed it back to him, "I believe this is yours, sir."

"Thank you!" He took the box and bowed.

Shi-ria bowed in return, "I suggest you contact your police before these hoodlums have a chance to escape."

"I already have," the shopkeeper assured her.

Shi-ria bowed once again and left. A few minutes later, the police were on the scene and had the Poison Starfish in custody. Detective Shinjo was on the scene questioning the shopkeeper. He told him everything that happened.

Shinjo pulled out a police sketch of Shi-ria and showed it to the shopkeeper, "Is this the woman?"

"Yes, that's her," he confirmed.

Just as I suspected! Shinjo thought. From the description the shopkeeper had given him, he had a feeling it was Shi-ria. For the past three weeks, Shinjo had been getting similar reports. Whether they be the Poison Starfish or random thugs attempting to commit petty crimes, many of them ended the same way: a mysterious woman with pink eyes and two pupils would show up, take the bad guys down with minimal effort, then disappear. Shinjo figured it had to be Shi-ria. Who else had pink eyes with two pupils in each? Shinjo couldn't help but be impressed with her combat skills.

He could still recall the incident at Teikoku City harbour from three months ago. He and his fellow officers were covertly watching the Poison Starfish smuggle ancient artifacts stolen from the Republic of Misr. The plan was for the police to move in and arrest them all once the deal was made. Everything suddenly went south when Shi-ria seemingly appeared right out of thin air. As if that wasn't weird enough, the artifacts themselves seemed to come to life and started attacking people, and then a group of nuns with guns showed up. Shinjo had been trying to explain all of this to his superiors. As a police detective, he always put the truth down in his reports, though even he had to admit that the whole incident sounded more like something out of a fantasy novel. Shinjo wasn't sure how or why, but he just knew Shi-ria was the key to all of this. If he found her, he'd find the answers he was looking for.

Shinjo returned to the police station and sat at his desk, going over the various reports. Ever since that night at the harbour, he had spent weeks trying to dig up as much information as he could on Shi-ria. He couldn't help but wonder about her pink eyes with two pupils in each. Was it some sort of genetic mutation? A birth defect? Was she one of these genetically enhanced "metamorphic humans," as they were called? Shinjo had heard rumours about a secret project that tried creating genetically enhanced humans who would supposedly have taken over the world and replaced all "normal" humans, only to have their operation foiled by a covert government team. Rumours about such things had been spreading around the world, dating back to almost sixty years. There were even rumours that such a project was later responsible for Earth's last world war about thirty years ago. Normally, Shinjo paid little attention to such rumours. As far as he was concerned, these were nothing more than crazy conspiracy theories by lunatics—the same lunatics who claimed the Earth was still flat, the moon landing was a hoax, and the Catholic Church had a secret military branch that went out hunting demons. Shinjo had always dismissed such crazy theories until that night when Shi-ria and those strange nuns interfered in his sting operation. While Shinjo's rational mind still insisted there had to be a logical explanation for all of this, a part of him—a very small part—couldn't help but wonder if maybe there was some grain of truth to those rumours. That's why he had been looking for Shi-ria. He somehow knew that she'd give him the answers he was looking for. Unfortunately, his investigation turned up nothing. There was no record of a woman even matching her description. It was as if this woman hadn't existed until that night; it was as though she literally just popped into existence right before his eyes.

No, he thought, *there must be a rational explanation for all of this*. Yet despite all his efforts to find her, his work had all been for nothing. Shinjo rubbed his eyes and looked over at the clock on his desk. It was after nine. He decided it was time to go home and get some sleep. He could tackle this mystery again tomorrow.

Location: A Public Park, Teikoku City

Shinjo was walking home when a strange man approached him. The man pulled out a small knife and held it up in front of Shinjo.

"You!" the man demanded. "Hand over your wallet!"

Shinjo stopped in his tracks. "Who are you?" he demanded.

"That's not important," the mugger countered. "I said HAND OVER YOUR WALLET NOW!"

"Look, you don't want to do this," Shinjo tried to explain, "I'm a cop."

If Shinjo thought that would convince his would-be mugger to stop or intimidate him into surrendering, he was in for a rude awakening, "Well, that's too bad, 'cause I've been arrested by the cops before. I don't like cops!"

"Well, to be perfectly honest, you have no one to blame but yourself for that," a familiar female voice said to the mugger. Shinjo and the mugger both turned to see Shi-ria appear from behind a nearby tree. "When you steal, it's inevitable that sooner or later, the authorities will come after you."

Seeing the mugger distracted, Shinjo made his move. He reached over and grabbed the man by his wrist, twisting it to make him drop the knife. Unfortunately, the mugger simply turned back to Shinjo, and with his free hand, punched him in the stomach. Shinjo released his grip on the mugger, who promptly turned and fled. Unfortunately for him, he didn't realize this mysterious woman was a Taman Knight. Using her Taman powers, Shi-ria leapt up in the air several feet, landing right in front of the mugger, forcing him to stop dead in his tracks. The mugger was dumbstruck. He left both this woman and the cop behind when he started running, yet she managed to jump up and over him, landing right in his path when she should have been scrambling to chase after him.

Shi-ria simply flashed him a smug grin, "It would be greatly appreciated if you were to surrender yourself to the authorities, sir." Instead, the mugger simply swung his knife at Shi-ria. However, thanks to her Taman abilities guiding her, she was effortlessly able to dodge all his wild attacks. Thus, she continually dodged while the mugger grew more desperate, swinging his blade wildly in the vain hope that he might land a blow. Shi-ria could sense the fear, anger, and frustration growing in him while Shi-ria, by contrast, remained calm and collected. Using her Taman alchemy, she focused on the knife, breaking down the metal blade, atom by atom. Thus, as the mugger made another desperate thrust, Shi-ria grabbed his wrist and held it up in front of him. The mugger watched in both horror and disbelief as the blade of his knife seemed to disintegrate right before his very eyes. He stared at

Shi-ria with a look of dread. Shi-ria simply smiled back at him and held his arm firmly in place.

Meanwhile, Shinjo had recovered from his blow and ran over to the two of them. Grabbing the mugger's free arm, he twisted it behind his back. Shi-ria did the same with the mugger's other arm. With both his arms restrained, Shinjo led the man over to a nearby tree and pressed him up against it, making sure he couldn't move. "You're under arrest!" he told the mugger before turning his attention to Shi-ria. "It's you!" Just when he decided to call it a day, go home, and get some rest, just as he put the case of Shi-ria on hold for the night, he found himself about to be mugged only for this mysterious woman to appear and take down his would-be mugger. While Shinjo wasn't normally a spiritual man, he couldn't help but wonder if fate had brought her to him again, like it did that night at the harbour.

"Yes, it's me," she said, bowing politely. "Forgive my lack of formality. My name is Shi-ria. No doubt you remember me from the incident at the harbour that night."

"Not exactly something I'd forget," Shinjo replied. "Wait! We're talking! How . . . I mean . . . last time we met, you . . . you were talking gibberish!"

"I'm actually speaking Thalien," Shi-ria explained. "My friend Mystic, the witch from Aryavarta, cast a translation spell on me. Whenever

I speak in my native tongue, whoever is listening to me hears my words in their native tongue. Just as when you speak to me in your language, I hear your words in my native Thalien."

Shinjo thought over what she was saying. It sounded crazy, "So, your friend . . . Mystic? This woman is a witch? From Aryavarta?" Shinjo recalled the events from the harbour. After he and his fellow officers retreated to a safe distance, he watched the whole incident unfold. He remembered seeing Shi-ria get shot by one of the nuns. Then a woman and man, who judging by their appearance, were obviously from Aryavarta, suddenly appeared in a swirling vortex of yellow mist. He recalled how the man seemed to open some portal into another part of the world, obviously, the Republic of Misr, as Shinjo recognized the pyramids from his studies in school. He then took those demons with him, no doubt returning them to their home while the woman tended to Shi-ria's wounds. Shinjo recalled how the nuns turned their weapons on Mystic only for her to seemingly yank them right out of their hands despite never touching them and made them magically hover in the air before departing with Shi-ria the same way she arrived.

"Yes," Shi-ria confirmed.

Figures, Shinjo thought. *If this Mystic could teleport at will and perform telekinesis, then she could probably use magic to translate languages without a problem instantly.* "You'll have to come with me too, ma'am," Shinjo told Shi-ria.

"Am I in trouble too?" Shi-ria asked. She wasn't angry or even upset that he appeared to be arresting her for helping him. Her reaction was one of confusion. "Am I to assume this is about the incident back at the harbour three months ago?"

Shinjo nodded. "I need to ask you a few questions about what happened back there."

Location: Police Station, Teikoku City, Oyashima, Earth

Shi-ria sat in a wooden chair at a table in the interrogation room. She shifted, trying to find a slightly more comfortable position. Shinjo had brought her in for questioning. After her unexpected arrival that night in Teikoku City harbour, there were many burning questions both Shinjo and the police force had for her. Unfortunately, things hadn't been going as well as any of them anticipated. Shinjo's superior sat across from her, grilling her relentlessly, while Shinjo stood back and watched silently. Shi-ria had been truthful and told them everything that happened that night, including being brought to Earth by Zolida, while Scarlet Knightwalker tried to send her home. Not to mention the fact that the notorious mercenary, Dead-Eye Sammie, was also brought to Earth and on the loose. Shinjo's superior wasn't buying it and kept asking her the same questions repeatedly, hoping she'd break down and confess the truth, not realizing that was exactly what she was doing.

"As I already explained, I am a Taman Knight from the planet Thalia. I was brought here to this planet against my will by a woman named Zolida. She insisted that I meet a witch named Mystic, her sorcerer husband Noonien, a demon named Tokijin, and a nun named Sister Valerie Rose. She then teleported me to the harbour, where you and your officers were waiting to arrest those criminals for their smuggling operation." Shi-ria could sense both confusion and frustration coming from them, though more from Shinjo's superior than Shinjo himself. Even without her Taman senses telling her this, it was obvious by the looks on their faces that they didn't believe her.

"And why did this Zolida want you to meet these people?" Shinjo's superior asked, growing more frustrated.

"You'll have to ask her," Shi-ria repeated. "She didn't bother to explain."

"And why did she send you into the middle of the Poison Starfish smuggling operation?" he demanded.

"Perhaps she thought Sister Rose would be there. As you already know, those artifacts they were smuggling were possessed by demons." She turned to Shinjo, "You were there; you saw it with your own eyes."

Shinjo's superior leaned back in his chair and rubbed his nose. He was getting tired of going around in circles. Shinjo simply stood behind, sheepishly nodding. He had witnessed the whole thing, so he had to admit she had a point. He had tried to find another, more rational explanation for what happened that night, but he couldn't find one. He looked in Shi-ria's eyes, and she looked back into his. Staring directly into her, Shinjo's gut told him that she was telling the truth, or at least she believed what she said to be the truth. As he stared into her eyes, another question came to him—a question he'd been wondering ever since he got a look at her eyes. "Excuse me, Ms. Shi-ria, but may I ask what is the deal with your eyes? I see you have two pupils per eye. Not to mention your eyes are pink."

"Pink is a common eye colour on my world."

"The planet Thalia?"

"Yes," she confirmed. "As for the two pupils, that is also common for Thaliens. Does it bother you?"

Her question caught Shinjo off guard. He had simply assumed it was a genetic mutation or birth defect. He didn't want to come across as though he was drawing unwanted attention to such a thing. "No . . . it doesn't bother me," he stammered, trying to come up with an answer that wouldn't offend her, "it's just . . . well . . . here on Earth, we don't normally see such . . . things." He paused for a moment before adding, "I'm sorry if I offended you."

"I assure you that I am not offended," Shi-ria soothed, sensing she was making him feel uncomfortable. "As a Taman Knight, I've learned that words can't hurt me, so why should I take offence by your curiosity?"

"What exactly are the Taman Knights?" Shinjo asked.

"We are a religious order from the planet Thalia," Shi-ria explained. "We are guardians of peace and justice on our world. We devote our lives to protecting the innocent and helping those in need."

"Is that why you've been showing up wherever there's a crime going on and taking down criminals?"

"Yes. I believe we all have a responsibility to help those who can't help themselves. To protect those who can't protect themselves. But more than that, I believe in a fundamental respect for all living beings. In my religion, we are all one with the Taman—the energy and will of the universe. We are all connected. We are all luminous beings temporarily encased in these physical bodies, but the truth is we are all part of the vast cosmic energy that is the Taman. Thus, by robbing from others, we are, in essence, robbing from ourselves. By hurting others, we are hurting ourselves."

Shinjo nodded. He had heard such beliefs before from branches of Hinduism, Buddhism, and Sikhism, although he never gave it much thought.

His superior stood up. Unlike Shinjo, it was obvious he was losing his patience. "This is all very fascinating," he made no attempt to hide his sarcasm, "but this isn't a class on theology. Now, let's take it from the top."

Shi-ria stared at him confused, "The top of what?"

"Name," he demanded.

"My name is still Shi-ria," she replied. "I assure you that it hasn't changed."

"You play games with me, lady, and you're through!"

"I'm through? Then may I leave now?"

Shinjo's superior facepalmed.

Shinjo decided it was time to step in, "What my superior is saying is that he doesn't believe your story, so he wants to start all over again."

"Oh, my apologies." Shi-ria bowed and added, "I misunderstood your words. However, if you don't believe my story, I don't see the point in continuing this interrogation. As a Taman Knight, I believe in being honest with people. However, if you prefer me to simply tell you what you want to hear, then I would ask you to give me the answers you wish me to respond with."

Shinjo put his hand over his mouth. He was trying not to laugh. He didn't get the feeling that she was being dishonest, nor did he feel she was being snarky. She legitimately didn't seem to grasp his superior's sarcasm and frustration. In any other situation, this might be humorous, but he knew his superior wasn't in the mood for comedy. Thus, he made some grumbling noises in his throat, trying to hide his laughter by making it look like he was trying to suppress a cough.

Just then, another woman entered the room, escorted by a uniformed police officer. "This is Ms. Kobayashi," the officer introduced her to the others. "She is both this woman's cousin and her attorney."

Shinjo, his superior, and Shi-ria looked at the woman. She had long black hair tied up in a bun and wore a business suit. She appeared to be an ordinary woman from Oyashima. Little did any of them know that it was Scarlet Knightwalker in disguise. Having used her magic to find and covertly keep an eye on Shi-ria, she witnessed Shi-ria stop Shinjo's mugger and then be brought into the station for interrogation. While Shi-ria didn't know it was Knightwalker, she could sense magical essence surrounding her, just like she had when she first encountered Knightwalker three months ago. However, she also sensed something else from this woman, but she wasn't quite certain what it was.

"I apologize for any trouble my cousin may have caused you," Ms. Kobayashi bowed. "It seems her condition is worse than we thought."

"Her condition?" Shinjo asked.

"My cousin over here is a novelist," she lied. "Her story about being a Thalien coming to Earth to meet with demons and witches; it's the plot of a fantasy novel she's been writing for the past few years. She's been trying to get it published, but she's been rejected by every publisher she's submitted it to. She's been so desperate to get it published it's . . . well . . ." Ms. Kobayashi lowered her head sheepishly, ". . . she's gone mad. She now believes herself to be this . . . Taman Knight character. She's hallucinating, officers. She's convinced that she's the titular character of this story." Shi-ria sat there silently. She knew none of this was true but felt it best to play along. She let the Taman guide her, telling her to go along with whatever this woman was planning. Suddenly, it dawned on her that this woman was Knightwalker in disguise.

"Then why did she interfere in our sting operation at the harbour that night?" Shinjo's superior demanded.

"An unfortunate coincidence," Ms. Kobayashi explained. "Her character helps fight crime like a superhero. In her delusional state, she just happened to be at the scene of the crime when your operation took place."

"And what about her appearing in a beam of light?" Shinjo asked.

"Special effects," Ms. Kobayashi explained. "Like the kind used in film and television productions."

"And the nuns? Or the demonic artifacts?" Shinjo asked, not entirely convinced.

"I assure you, those events didn't actually happen," she insisted. "It was all simply an illusion."

Typically, Shinjo and his fellow police officers wouldn't believe such an obvious ruse, but none knew they were dealing with Knightwalker. As for her excuses to explain away the strange events that transpired at the harbour, she had a small potion bottle, disguised as a bottle of perfume, which she applied to herself while waiting to see her "cousin." While not causing complete mind control, this potion let anyone who got a whiff of it to become susceptible to suggestion. Thus, it didn't matter whether the police truly believed her story or not. In their current state, she could have told them that both she and Shi-ria were simply figments of their imaginations, and the police would have believed it. While Knightwalker didn't like having to trick the police in this manner, she had little choice under the circumstances. If they didn't believe Shi-ria's story, they wouldn't believe her either, and the last thing Knightwalker wanted was to reveal the truth to the police. Finding out beings with magic powers were bringing aliens to Earth would cause panic and hysteria. As far as Knightwalker was concerned, the people of Earth were nowhere near ready for the revelation that many more advanced civilizations and planets were out there. Thus, her plan was to simply get the police to release Shi-ria into her custody so that she could bring her home before the potion wore off. By which time both she and Shi-ria would be gone, and the police would have another unsolved case that would be filed away and eventually forgotten.

"That would explain everything," Shinjo, under the influence of the potion, concluded.

"There's still the fact that your cousin interfered in our operation," his superior added.

"I'm terribly sorry for any trouble she caused you," Ms. Kobayashi bowed. "If you would be so kind as to turn my cousin over to me, I shall take her to a hospital to see that she gets the proper treatment she so desperately needs."

Shi-ria noted how the two officers seemed to suddenly be willing to accept her story as the truth, despite the obvious holes in it. Even Shi-ria found a small part of herself starting to believe it. That's when the Taman again showed her what was going on. Ever since Ms. Kobayashi entered the room, Shi-ria noticed a sweet scent coming from her. At first, she simply dismissed it as the perfume she was wearing, but now she recognized the magic potion. Shi-ria had seen this before; petty criminals had used such potions to convince people to hand over money and other valuables to them before. No wonder the police suddenly seemed so eager to dismiss the whole incident. Had it not been for Shi-ria's Taman senses, she would probably be under the same influence as the police.

Under the influence of the potion as well, Shinjo's superior changed his tone from irritation to that of calm understanding. "Very well, Ms. Kobayashi, we'll leave her in your care. I hope you can help your cousin."

"Thank you, officers; I shall do everything I can." She bowed to them politely before turning to address Shi-ria, "Come, Shi-ria, let's get you back home to your planet."

"As you wish, cousin." Shi-ria stood up, playing along. She wasn't sure if Knightwalker would send her home or whether this was simply part of her act, but this was not the time or place to debate the matter. Shi-ria then turned to face both Shinjo and his superior, "I'm sorry for any trouble I may have caused you," she said, bowing respectfully. "Goodnight, gentlemen."

"Goodnight." Both Shinjo and his superior bowed as the junior officer escorted the two women out of the room. Shinjo and his superior were now alone in the room, or at least they thought they were. Neither of them knew there was another person, someone who had secretly been there all along: Zolida. Like Knightwalker, Zolida, too, had used her magic to watch the whole incident. However, unlike Knightwalker who used her magic staves to create the illusion of Ms. Kobayashi, Zolida simply cast an invisibility spell on herself. She had been standing in the room the whole time, and no one had noticed her—not even Knightwalker or Shi-ria had sensed her presence with their powers. Now, Zolida was going to make her move. With Shinjo and his superior still under the effects of Knightwalker's potion, Zolida decided to add a touch of her own magic to it.

"Something doesn't seem right," she whispered, her words flowing directly into Shinjo's mind.

"Something doesn't seem right," Shinjo repeated, unaware that Zolida was manipulating him like a puppet.

"I thought so too!" Zolida replied, reaching out with her magic to take control of his superior's mind. "Follow them! Find out what's really going on!"

Like Shinjo, his superior was under her control without realizing it. "I thought so too!" he repeated her words, thinking they were his own. "Follow them! Find out what's really going on!"

"Yes, sir." And with that, Shinjo turned and walked out the door, preparing to covertly follow Shi-ria and Knightwalker. His superior turned and walked back to his office. Zolida was now alone in the room.

All too easy! she thought to herself.

***

Shi-ria and Ms. Kobayashi left the station and started walking down the street. Not too far behind, but far enough to keep out of their sight, walked Shinjo. He was being very careful to make sure that they didn't see him. Although he didn't realize it, he was also getting help from Zolida. Since Shi-ria or Knightwalker were no ordinary humans, even if Shinjo managed to keep himself hidden from their sight, Shi-ria with her Taman senses and Knightwalker with her magic staves would have alerted them to the fact that someone was covertly following them. Zolida used her magic to make sure that this wouldn't happen. After several minutes, Shi-ria and Ms. Kobayashi walked into a remote corner of a nearby public park, heading off the pathway and near a group of trees, away from the lampposts where they could be certain no one would see them—no one except for Detective Shinjo and Zolida. Shinjo stealthily moved behind a tree, then ducked behind some bushes nearby, making sure neither of them could see him. Zolida, still invisible, simply stood in front of the bushes watching. Were it not for her invisibility spell, she would've been blocking Shinjo's view, not to mention both Shi-ria and Knightwalker would have seen her standing right there watching. Thanks to her magic, neither of them could sense her or Shinjo.

"Now, Ms. Kobayashi, perhaps you'd like to tell me who you really are," Shi-ria said.

"Very well." She removed her magic disguise, revealing her true self.

"Scarlet Knightwalker."

"You knew?"

"I had a feeling," Shi-ria admitted. "I assume you're here to send me back to Thalia?"

"Yes."

"First, I have a few questions. Why did Zolida bring me here to Earth? And why are you so determined to send me home?"

"I can't tell you that."

"Why?"

"Because . . ." Knightwalker's voice trailed off. She had been debating this ever since Shi-ria first arrived on Earth. Should she tell her the truth? How she's destined to find an apprentice, train her, then die and have her apprentice turn evil? It seemed cruel to reveal such a horrible future to her. However, was it right to keep her in the dark? Shi-ria did have a point; she was brought to Earth against her will by Zolida. She did have a right to know why. After all, if it had been the other way around—if Knightwalker had been brought to this world against her will—she too would want to know why. ". . . because I'm from the future."

Shi-ria stopped and stared. Her Taman senses normally gave her limited precognitive abilities, so there was very little that surprised her, but this revelation was one that genuinely caught her off guard. She wanted to say something, but no words came to her.

"I've seen what will happen, Ms. Shi-ria." Knightwalker continued, "You will find a teenage girl and take her as your apprentice. Then you'll die, and she'll become a Koldar Warrior and cause massive suffering."

Shi-ria recalled when Tokijin suggested Zolida brought her to Earth as part of some prophecy to stop "the one who was not of this Earth." She recalled how she used her precognitive abilities to see the future. "I did foresee one such future. Where I did die, along with Noonien and Tokijin," Shi-ria admitted. "However, I also saw another one. One where the three of us survive and my apprentice becomes a Taman Knight."

"Not in the future I came from," Knightwalker snapped.

"Is that why you don't want me here?" Shi-ria asked. "You're trying to prevent your future from happening?"

Knightwalker nodded.

"And am I correct to assume that Zolida brought me here to ensure the future unfolds just as you've seen?"

"Yes," Knightwalker confirmed. "That's why Zolida brought you here, to keep me from altering the future any further."

"Any further?" Shi-ria inquired. "Have you already changed history?"

Knightwalker nodded again. "Do you recall five years ago when you were still an apprentice? The Koldar Warriors kidnapped your sister Kurai. They tried to turn her, to make her succumb to her inner darkness."

"Yes, I remember," Shi-ria recalled the incident vividly. Shi-ria, her "sister" Kurai, and her "brother" Rirk were orphans growing up on the streets of the city of Kalshiya. While Rirk and Kurai weren't technically brother and sisters, at least not in the biological sense, the three had known each other as far back as any of them could remember. Being orphans, they were the closest thing Shi-ria had to a family. In every sense, they were her brother and sister. She loved them as if they were her biological siblings and would do anything—even sacrifice her own life—to save them. When they were still small children, they were caught stealing food from some street vendors. The vendors were prepared to beat the three of them to death for their crimes. Had it not been for the timely intervention of their master,

Kalai-Udon, the vendors might have very well ended their lives right then and there. Instead, Kalai-Udon took the three of them in and trained them as Taman Knights.

Shi-ria's memories then turned to the incident from five years ago, which Knightwalker spoke of. While on a goodwill mission, Shi-ria, Rirk, Kurai, and Master Kalai had been ambushed by a group of Koldar Warriors who believed themselves to be the true Taman Knights and that the current, legitimate branches of the Taman Knights had distorted the teachings of the original Taman Knights. Shi-ria recalled how this cult consisted of followers of the late Master Daisho, a Taman Knight of the Alderoth sect that started a Taman civil war long ago when he launched an attack against his fellow Taman master, Kamatra. Master Kamatra felt the Alderoth branch of the Taman Knights was wrong in forbidding emotional attachment, pointing out that while love could lead to jealousy, denying it simply made it that much more appealing to apprentices. When he encouraged others to question the teachings of the Alderoth sect, he was banished for this, resulting in the creation of the Kamatra sect, the branch of the Taman Knights Shi-ria, Rirk, Kurai, and Master Kalai-Udon belonged to. According to history, Master Daisho took Kamatra's actions as "heresy" and accused him of falling to the Koldar. As a result, Master Daisho developed an obsession with destroying the Kamatra sect. Master Daisho was later expelled from the Taman Knights on the orders of the Thalien government. He and some of his followers formed their own branch who became Koldar Warriors, and because their desire to destroy this "evil" was so strong, it caused them to become the very thing they sought to destroy. Shi-ria recalled how the Alderoth sect covered this up to avoid a public scandal. When she, Master Kalai, Rirk, and Kurai informed the Alderoth sect about this cult, they dismissed this and tried to accuse Kurai, who had been having visions of these past events, of trying to slander their branch of the Taman Knights.

Shi-ria recalled how angry Kurai became at such an accusation. Both being hot-headed teenagers at the time, Shi-ria taunted Kurai, which in turn caused her to lose her temper and nearly kill Shi-ria in a fit of rage. Shi-ria recalled sensing such blinding rage coming from her sister and how it filled her with fear. Shi-ria could still recall the teachings of the Alderoth sect and how fear leads to anger and hate. Shi-ria became afraid of losing Kurai to the Koldar, but she also feared herself giving in to it. Her master's wise words reminded her that fear can be good in that it reminds one of danger and protects one from being reckless, for recklessness was one of Shi-ria's problems as an apprentice. She had a nasty habit of rushing into situations without thinking. In fact, many of her fellow apprentices nicknamed Shi-ria "the fearless fool." Shi-ria remembered that this very cult had abducted Kurai with the intent of turning her into a Koldar Warrior. Shi-ria felt a huge sense of guilt over this. Fearing that she would have been the one who drove her sister to the Koldar Warriors, she was determined to save Kurai at all costs.

"I'll never forget that incident," she said, her voice still carrying a twinge of regret.

"The Koldar Warriors were trying to find the same ancient spell that Zolida used to bring you to Earth," Knightwalker explained. "Their goal was to use that spell to launch attacks all over the galaxy so that they could force their religious beliefs across the galaxy and destroy all 'infidels' who didn't share their views. In your haste to save Kurai from this cult, they ended up using this spell to send you to Earth by accident. While your Master and the other Taman Knights showed up and stopped them before they could use it again, it was too late to rescue you. The Taman Knights believed you had been killed in the incident. They didn't know that you were here on Earth."

Shi-ria pondered Knightwalker's words. That would explain why she was determined to alter history. It was after those events that Shi-ria truly began to grow from that reckless, impulsive, "fearless fool" into the more calm, rational, and mature woman she was today. If that immature child had been sent to Earth instead of remaining on Thalia, finishing her training and graduating to a full-fledged Taman Knight; if that reckless fool had taken an apprentice, while she herself was still technically an apprentice, then said apprentice would have grown to be a reckless, irresponsible, foolish Taman Knight who might have easily given in to anger and become a Koldar Warrior.

"I now see why you didn't wish me to come to Earth," Shi-ria conceded.

"Then you see why you must return to Thalia."

"Unfortunately, there's still the matter of the mercenary," Shi-ria reminded her. "When Zolida brought me here, she also brought Dead-Eye."

"I haven't forgotten," Knightwalker added ruefully.

"I was sent to prevent him from stealing relics from a cave on Thalia," Shi-ria recalled her original mission. A group of archaeologists found some relics dating back to the time of the original Taman Knights over a thousand years ago—relics that would be worth lots of money on the black market. Shi-ria was acting as a security guard, trying to stop Dead-Eye from stealing them when they were both brought to Earth by Zolida. "There's also the matter of my apparent involvement in the prophecy."

"Prophecy?"

"Surely you're aware of it," Shi-ria looked Knightwalker directly in the eyes. Ordinarily, she'd be able to sense what someone was feeling, but she couldn't sense anything from Knightwalker. All she could gather from her eyes was what appeared to be confusion. "The prophecy that I'm supposed to be a part of. 'The descendant of the darkness will cause the shadows to rise, and darkness shall envelop the world. Then the one who is not of this world will seek out the true light within the darkness, and the shadows will open the gates to the netherworld. The true light will shine, removing all shadows from the world while the Earth seals the shadows within the netherworld for all eternity.'"

Knightwalker simply stared at Shi-ria. Her eyes hinted at no emotion, no feelings other than confusion.

"You said you're from the future," Shi-ria continued. "Did you not witness this prophecy? Did it not come true?"

Knightwalker searched her memories. They were a long time ago, even for Knightwalker. Though, as far as anyone else was concerned, those events she recalled hadn't happened yet. Digging deep through her mind, Knightwalker recalled how Shi-ria's apprentice, Valerie Rose, and Mystic were part of a team of "heroes" on a mission to protect humanity. However, their mission had become to protect humanity from itself. They claimed that humanity had proven themselves too irresponsible to handle governing themselves, too immature to handle such "privileges" like freedom of speech, freedom of the press, and the right to demonstrate. Thus, protecting humanity meant turning the planet into a totalitarian dictatorship, which they ruled with an iron fist.

Knightwalker could still recall how she and her friends had been liberated by a group of freedom fighters who chose to stand up against Earth's so-called "protectors." Yet, she never recalled anything about a prophecy. Nor did she ever witness or even hear of this "descendant of the darkness." It was possible that in Knightwalker's future, this person was also working to fight Mystic, Rose, and the others, or it was possible that this event had already transpired, and Knightwalker was simply unaware of it as it was not important at the time. However, it was also possible that such an event may not have yet occurred. Knightwalker could only shake her head. "I'm sorry, Ms. Shi-ria, but I know nothing of this prophecy you speak of. If this event has transpired . . ." Knightwalker stopped herself mid-sentence. She had to remind herself that while from her perspective these events already happened, from everyone else's point of view, none of these things happened yet. ". . . if this even *is to* transpire . . ." she corrected herself, ". . . then from my point of view, it hasn't yet occurred."

"Then I may still be needed here," Shi-ria pointed out.

"And what if by remaining, you end up causing the very future we both wish to avoid?"

"You have already altered the future, Scarlet Knightwalker," Shi-ria pointed out. "Things have already changed, as you pointed out yourself. The future I experience may very well be different than the one you encountered."

"And if it isn't?"

"Are you familiar with the law of attraction?"

Knightwalker thought it over but ultimately shrugged her shoulders. "No," she confessed.

"The law of attraction says that 'like attracts like,'" Shi-ria explained.

"I'm sorry, Ms. Shi-ria," Knightwalker shrugged, "but I don't see how . . ."

"In other words, your thoughts create your reality," Shi-ria explained, figuring that Knightwalker was going to ask how it pertains to their current situation. "When a person thinks about what they don't have, for example, they say 'I want more money,' the universe responds in kind by giving more of the feeling of *wanting* money, not actually having it. In other words, the more you think about trying to prevent the future you *don't* want, the more the universe responds in kind by giving you the very future you wish to avoid."

"The universe gives me what I *don't* want?" Knightwalker asked doubtfully.

"The universe, God, the Taman—call it whatever you like," Shi-ria continued. "The point is, it doesn't understand words like 'don't.' While you may be *saying* you don't want this future to happen, the universe or God or whatever sees you're constantly thinking about this future, so it responds in kind and gives you more of the same, the very future you wish to avoid." Knightwalker thought it over. A part of her thought such an idea was preposterous, yet a part of her also thought it made some sense. Many people often claimed that their prayers went unanswered. The law of attraction would then explain why. Like Shi-ria said, if people prayed for what they didn't have, then their claim that their prayers went unanswered was simply the law of attraction giving them more of what they already had, or more feelings of *wanting* that which they didn't. But this was hardly the time or place to debate such matters.

"So what you're saying is that the more I try and prevent this future from happening, the more I ensure that it will happen, correct?"

"Exactly," Shi-ria confirmed.

Meanwhile, Zolida and Shinjo were still secretly watching all of this. Shinjo was hiding behind some bushes next to a nearby tree, while Zolida stood in front of him, still invisible and undetected. She decided this was the perfect time to act. "Well, then I suppose the correct thing to do is to let you keep doing what you're doing, Scarlet," Zolida called out before she removed her invisibility spell, appearing directly in front of Shinjo. Shinjo was caught completely off guard by this. Thanks to Zolida's spell, he had no idea she had been following him, nor did he realize that she had been covertly manipulating him. He staggered backwards, failing to notice part of the exposed tree root directly behind him. Thus, the sound of him falling backwards alerted both Knightwalker and Shi-ria to his presence.

"Detective Shinjo!" Shi-ria shouted. She, too, was caught completely off guard. Her Taman senses normally allowed her to sense when she was being followed, but she hadn't noticed him at all this time. Turning her attention to Zolida, Shi-ria quickly deduced that she was responsible for this.

"Yes, I was the one who cast the spell to block your ability to sense both his presence and my own." Zolida answered the question she knew they were going to ask. "I used it to hide right in front of you all."

"So you were in the police station the whole time," Knightwalker deduced.

"I was." She motioned toward Shinjo and said, "I was also the one who convinced our detective friend here to follow you."

Shinjo got to his feet. "All right, all of you! I want some answers now! What's going on here? Who are you people?"

Zolida didn't answer; instead, she turned to face Scarlet Knightwalker. "You've shown me the error of my ways, Scarlet." Despite her words, her tone made it obvious that she didn't mean it. Like an actor intentionally hamming it up, the only way she could have made it more obvious would be if she were to come right out and state that she was lying. "So, I'm here to make up for my past mistakes." With a wave of her hands, a shield appeared around her, Shi-ria, and Shinjo. The only one left outside was Knightwalker.

"What are you doing?" Knightwalker demanded.

"Exactly what you wanted me to do," Zolida smugly replied. Using her magic, Zolida used the same incantation she originally used to bring Shi-ria to Earth. Shi-ria tried to move, but she couldn't. Zolida was also using her magic to hold her in place. Shi-ria felt just like she had back in the cave on Thalia. Zolida's powers were such that she could somehow block Shi-ria's Taman senses. To make matters worse, Shinjo was also caught in the same spell. He couldn't move as well.

"What's going on?" he demanded.

"You didn't believe her story," Zolida explained. "Shi-ria told you she was an alien from another planet, and you thought she was some sort of lunatic. Now you're gonna find out the truth."

"Zolida, STOP!" Knightwalker shouted.

"Why?" Zolida asked. "This is what you wanted, isn't it?" Zolida resumed her incantation while Knightwalker pulled out two magic staves. Last time, she tried blasting through Zolida's shield, but it proved futile. This time, she tried to use their magic to spread through the ground. Hopefully, her magic could come up from underneath the shield. Knightwalker hoped she could knock Zolida out, stop her from casting the spell and make her drop the shield. Knightwalker wasn't so much worried about Shi-ria being sent home; she was more worried about Shinjo. Thanks to Zolida, not only had Shi-ria come to Earth, not only had she ensured that the future Knightwalker was so desperately trying to prevent could still happen, not only had Zolida also brought Dead-Eye Sammie, one of the most notorious mercenaries in the galaxy, to this world, now she was about to send an Earthling to an alien world.

Muttering an incantation of her own, Knightwalker activated her two staves. Crossing them in an X pattern, two small red lines of pure energy—one from each staff—moved out from the bottom of each staff along the ground before meeting directly in the middle. Forming one larger red line, it shot out in the direction of Zolida's shield. However, Zolida anticipated this. As soon as the line of energy hit the shield, it seemed to explode on contact. Sparks of orange energy sprayed out in all directions. The force was so much that it knocked Knightwalker off her feet. She was flung backwards, her two staves flying out of her hands and landing harmlessly on the ground to either side of her.

"Trying to attack from underneath my shield, Scarlet?" Zolida taunted. "Did you really think my shield only extended from the ground up? Did you think I wouldn't anticipate this? That I'd be foolish enough not to extend the barrier under the ground too? I guess I shouldn't be surprised. After all, you're not really a true mage; you're just a cripple with a few magically-imbued crutches!"

Knightwalker got back to her feet. "ZOLIDA, NO!" But it was too late, like that night three months ago. A glowing pentagram surrounded by two circles with a ring of runes between them appeared on the ground directly beneath Shi-ria, Shinjo, and Zolida. The blinding light emanating from this caused everyone except Zolida to shield their eyes. When the light faded, Knightwalker looked to see she was alone. *What have you done, Zolida?* she thought.

LOCATION: HEADQUARTERS OF THE TAMAN KNIGHTS, PLANET THALIA

Shi-ria looked around; she immediately recognized where she was. She was back home at the Headquarters of the Taman Knights. It was made of stone, carved out of the cliffs of the side of a mountain. Yet despite its ancient look, inside, they had access to the same modern technologies and facilities one would expect to find in any city on Thalia. The temple was divided into various dorms where Taman Knights and apprentices lived, classrooms where students could learn about the Taman, gymnasiums and outdoor courtyards for exercise and practising their martial arts skills. In addition, there was a mess hall where they would gather for meals and a huge library which Shi-ria had visited with Mystic about a week after she had been brought to Earth—the library where they attempted to find any information they could on either Zolida or Scarlet Knightwalker. And, of course, there was also the council chamber room. This was where Mystic and Shi-ria went to inform the Taman council about what had happened three months ago. When their attempt to learn about Zolida and Scarlet Knightwalker was cut short due to Noonien's old fiancé, Aanjay, and Tokijin's adversary, Jimomaru, they attempted to turn Tokijin and Sister Rose against one another, first by putting Tokijin in mortal danger and forcing Rose to choose between the Order of the Cross and her love, then later by placing Tokijin under and spell and forcing him to attack Sister Rose.

Indeed, a lot had happened to Shi-ria in the three months since she last stood in these sacred halls. She couldn't help but feel a slight sense of unease. If Zolida could use her magic to instantly teleport anyone anywhere in the galaxy, and since there was no record of her and no one who knew who she was, that made her a potentially dangerous person.

Shinjo looked around; he had no idea where he was. Just a few minutes ago, it was late at night in Teikoku City. He was following Shi-ria and her "cousin" to find out what was going on, and the next thing he knew, he had been transported to a faraway place—a place he didn't recognize. He looked over at Shi-ria. While he didn't have her Taman abilities, he recognized the look on her face; it was obvious she knew where they were. This strange-looking temple was obviously familiar to her. It seemed to make her feel at ease. "Where are we?" he asked.

The sound of his voice seemed to snap her out of her daze, "Oh, I'm sorry, detective," she stammered, "I guess I was distracted. This is the temple of the Kamatra sect of the Taman Knights. This is my home."

". . . on the planet Thalia," Shinjo added. A part of him still believed what "Ms. Kobayashi" said. A part of him still couldn't accept that he was on an alien world on the other side of the galaxy. Yet, he had no rational explanation for what occurred.

Shi-ria could sense his confusion. She had been so engrossed by the fact that she was back home that she completely neglected to consider how Shinjo must have felt. It was just like when she was first brought to Earth, except in Shinjo's case, it had to be even worse. While Shi-ria knew very little of Earth, she at least knew it existed, and it had life. By the standards of Thalia, Earth was still primitive. Many people on Earth still believed their planet was the only one in the entire universe capable of supporting life. She imagined Shinjo had never believed in aliens, now to find himself on an alien world, to learn that everything he knew, he believed to be wrong. It would be overwhelming for any person. "I know this must be very difficult for you to accept, detective," she took his hand, trying to soothe him, "but I assure you that this isn't a dream or hallucination. You are on an alien planet in a different part of the galaxy. And I promise I'll bring you back home." Shi-ria suddenly stopped; she sensed a familiar presence approaching—one she recognized all too well.

"Shi-ria? Is that you?" a male voice spoke behind her. She turned around; there was another young Taman Knight, a man about her age. He was tall with a muscular, athletic build. He wore a long sleeveless red vest over a black short-sleeved shirt. His legs were covered by dark brown pants tucked into dark red boots, not unlike what Shi-ria wore. Over his hands and forearms were the same dark red gauntlets as Shi-ria. He had long black hair, combed back, which fell loose around his shoulders. His eyes were aqua-coloured, and like Shi-ria, he had two pupils per eye.

Shi-ria was very happy to see her "brother" again. "Rirk!" she grinned. The two of them approached each other and hugged. "It's good to see you again!"

"It's good to see you too!" he replied.

Shi-ria turned to face Shinjo and said, "This is my brother, Rirk." She introduced the two of them, "Rirk, this is detective Shinjo. He's from the planet Earth."

"It's a pleasure to meet you," Rirk said, bowing politely.

In turn, Shinjo bowed respectfully. However, his face showed confusion at his words. He assumed Rirk was offering some sort of greeting, but he wasn't sure.

Rirk could sense the confusion coming from Shinjo. He spoke, but Shinjo couldn't understand his language, just like Shi-ria when he first met her three months ago at the harbour.

"I'm sorry," Shinjo shrugged, "but I don't speak your language. I can't understand what you're saying."

Rirk stared at him in confusion. Shi-ria turned to Rirk and repeated Shinjo's words. She then turned to Shinjo. "Forgive me. I forgot about the translation spell Mystic used. The spell allows me to hear your words in my native Thalien and you to hear mine in your native language. But since the spell wasn't cast on you, you wouldn't be able to understand anyone else here. Just as they don't speak your language." She then turned to Rirk and explained it to him. Rirk, in turn, spoke to Shi-ria in Thalien. She nodded and turned back to Shinjo. "He said to follow him. He'll get you a translation device. It's a small piece of equipment similar to your planet's wireless headset. It will allow you to hear what others say in your native language while translating your words into Thalien."

Shinjo smiled and bowed toward Rirk. Then, the three of them went off. A few minutes later, Shinjo was fitted with the device. It was small, and it hooked over his left ear. He was now able to understand everything Rirk and the other Taman Knights said, just as they could now understand him. "Thank you, Mr. Rirk," Shinjo said, bowing.

Rirk bowed in return. "Welcome to Thalia, Mr. Shinjo." He then turned to Shi-ria, "Master Kalai-Udon explained to me what happened. For a while, Kurai and I feared you had been killed. Seeing you alive and well brings warm feelings to my heart!"

"Where is Kurai?" Shi-ria asked.

"She's been at the capital, meeting with politicians for the past few days," Rirk explained. "I expect her back any minute now."

"Kurai?" Shinjo asked.

"My wife," Rirk explained.

"My sister," Shi-ria added.

Shinjo gave them both a confused look. "She's *your* wife . . ." he pointed to Rirk, ". . . yet she's *your* sister . . ." he pointed to Shi-ria, ". . . and he's your brother. . ." he pointed back to Rirk while looking at Shi-ria, ". . . meaning Kurai is also *his* sister, but also *his wife*?"

Shi-ria and Rirk both chuckled at this. "Well, they're not *literally* my brother and sister . . ." Shi-ria explained, ". . . at least not in the biological sense."

"What she means is that the three of us grew up together," Rirk interjected. "Shi-ria, Kurai, and I were orphans from the city of Kalshiya. We had no families growing up. We lived on the streets, stealing whatever we needed to survive. The only thing we had was each other."

"Rirk and Kurai were the closest thing I had to family," Shi-ria explained.

"One day, we were caught stealing food from a group of street vendors," Rirk continued. "They would have killed us had it not been for the intervention of our master, Kalai-Udon."

"He brought us here and trained us as Taman Knights. Gave us a new home, a new life," Shi-ria said. "In a way, Rirk and Kurai are my brother and sister . . ."

"Just as Kurai and myself think of Shi-ria as ours," Rirk added.

". . . and Master Kalai is our father," she concluded.

Shinjo smiled and nodded, "I understand now."

Just then, another woman walked into the room. She was a foot shorter than Shi-ria. She had the same aqua-coloured eyes as Rirk and black hair as the rest of them. Her face was partially obscured by a maroon hooded cloak she wore over her light blue sleeveless tank top. She wore matching baggy blue trousers and brown leather sandals over her exposed toes. She pulled back the hood, letting her braided ponytail fall behind her neck. Like Shi-ria, she wore a red headband and had dark red gauntlets around her wrists and forearms, but unlike Shi-ria or Rirk, she had no gloves. It was Kurai. She looked over at Shi-ria and was stunned. She clearly wasn't expecting to see her.

"Shi-ria?" Kurai gasped.

"Hello, Kurai!" Shi-ria smiled back. The two moved closer and hugged.

"Master Kalai told Rirk and I that you were still alive. That you were sent to a planet called Earth by some sorceress."

"Yes," Shi-ria confirmed as she told her about Zolida, Knightwalker, and her adventures in the past three months.

"I see, so you've come home empty-handed and still haven't found Dead-Eye," Kurai mockingly teased. "I should've known you couldn't finish the job without us."

"Maybe you should come back to Earth with me," Shi-ria playfully retorted. "You can find Dead-Eye, then nag him until he surrenders."

Rirk just stood there, trying to suppress his laughter.

"What are you smirking at?" Kurai asked.

"Sorry, I must confess, a part of me missed hearing you two bickering all the time."

Both Shi-ria and Kurai tried to scowl, but even they couldn't help but find his words somewhat amusing. Kurai then turned her attention to Shinjo. "Detective Shinjo, I presume?"

"Yes," Shinjo bowed.

"Welcome to the planet Thalia," Kurai bowed in return.

"How did your meeting with the first minister go?" Rirk asked Kurai, changing the subject.

"We found out who was behind the theft of those artifacts," she explained.

Shinjo looked at her with surprise. For a moment, he thought Kurai was referring to the event that had transpired back at Teikoku City harbour. The three of them sensed his surprise. While neither Rirk nor Kurai understood, Shi-ria realized what Shinjo must have assumed.

"Before I was brought to Earth, I was assigned to guard some relics found in a cave here on Thalia," she explained. "Like the incident at the harbour, someone was stealing artifacts here too." She turned her attention back to Kurai and said, "Who was behind it?"

"Do you remember that cult that claimed they were the true followers of the Taman teachings?

That claimed we were the ones who perverted the teachings of Princess Alderoth?"

"Those who tried to get you to join them?"

"The very same," Kurai confirmed.

Shinjo just stood there confused. Sensing this, Shi-ria once again turned to him to explain.

"Forgive me," she apologized. "I suppose some backstory is required here: Over a thousand years ago, there was a princess named Alderoth. She grew up living a life of luxury and security, but as a small child when she went on a trip with her parents, they were ambushed by a group of nobles plotting to seize power. To protect their child, they told Alderoth to flee into the woods while they held off their attackers. What became of them is unknown, but it's assumed they were killed."

"While hiding in the woods, she came across a tribe living in a commune in the forests," Rirk continued. "They lived simple lives and often spent time meditating to hear the voice of nature, thus they were in tune with it. They took her in and raised her according to their traditions. She began to learn to live a simplistic life. Years later, she realized that her life of royalty and luxury had brought her life into chaos, and becoming part of this nature tribe finally brought balance to her life. As she grew up, she spent much of her adulthood wandering the forests, searching for enlightenment. One day, while meditating under a tree, she had a vision. She later described her vision in a group of scrolls that formed the basis of the Taman philosophy."

"So, this tribe, they were the first Taman Knights?" Shinjo asked.

"I suppose," Rirk admitted. "They were one of many tribes who had a special connection with nature and the universe. In a way, they were the precursors to our religion."

Kurai continued the story, "According to what she wrote down in her scrolls, Princess Alderoth described the 'voice of nature' and the life force around her as the 'energy and will of the universe.' She wrote down that the calming serenity or 'inner light,' the 'Kolri,' as we call it, is the only way to control greed, aggression, our 'inner darkness' or 'Koldar,' and maintain balance and harmony in the world. Thus, all beings must maintain this balance, which we call 'Taman.'"

Rirk took over, explaining, "Alderoth continued travelling Thalia as a healer, teaching others her beliefs. As she relied more on her instincts and used her connection with the universe, she began discovering inner powers she hadn't noticed before. After years of training and self-exploration, she discovered that people who use positive energy to control the negative energy within themselves could develop the powers now associated with the Taman Knights and use them to maintain peace and justice in the world. She trained several followers in this practice who continued passing on these teachings after she died."

"This led to the founding of the Taman Knights then," Shinjo concluded.

"Yes," Rirk nodded.

"Many of Alderoth's followers travelled around Thalia teaching others, who, in turn, taught others, thus leading to the start of the master/apprentice relationship that exists to this day." Shi-ria continued, "Studying movements based on animals and the natural elements of air, water, earth, and fire, the Taman knights had developed a form of exercise/meditation that eventually evolved into the form of martial arts. Just as you saw me perform." Shinjo recalled watching her take down the members of the Poison Starfish that night at the harbour and her subduing that mugger in the park earlier. "Being peaceful monks, these exercises were developed as a form of self-defence. As groups spread across different lands, different forms of teaching and martial arts developed. Eventually, these distant groups came together to form a united order dedicated to spreading the knowledge of the Taman. They developed a set of codes to follow, which are still in use today. Combining these writings with the writings of princess Alderoth, they wrote the book of Taman, which is the basis of our religious text." Shi-ria explained, "They used an old monastery as their headquarters, where they trained their students and spent their days meditating. They developed various weapons for training and combat and created three groups: the peacekeepers who maintained harmony and order, the healers who used their powers to heal the sick and injured, and the guards who defended the order from outside attacks. At first, they forged weapons but eventually learned the art of creating physical weapons and tools out of pure energy, which they dubbed Taman alchemy."

"How?" Shinjo asked.

"The universe is made of matter and energy," Shi-ria explained. "All matter is made of atoms, which are made of protons, neutrons, and electrons, which are made of quarks, which are energy. So this entire universe is one giant ocean of energy. This is what we call the Taman. Thus, by manipulating the atoms at the subatomic level, we can change matter and energy into different forms."

Shinjo looked at her with shock. "With such power, you're practically gods!"

Shi-ria chuckled, "Well, technically, we too are a part of the Taman. Now, if you think of the Taman, or this 'ocean of energy' as God, then all living beings are God. Everything from the most powerful wizards to the smallest microorganism. We are all God, including you, Detective Shinjo."

"That's the first time someone described me as a god," Shinjo laughed.

"As it says in your Earth bible," Shi-ria explained, "from the book of Exodus: *'And Moses said unto God, Behold, when I come unto the children of Israel, and shall say unto them, The God of your fathers hath sent me unto you; and they shall say to me, What is his name? What shall I say unto them? And God said unto Moses, I AM THAT I AM. And he said, Thus, shalt thou say unto the children of Israel, I AM hath sent me unto you.'* So, think about it, Who is God?"

Shinjo thought it over, "I am?"

Shi-ria nodded. "You are. So am I. And Rirk, and your superior, and every other living thing. And maybe her too." Shi-ria motioned toward Kurai, playfully teasing her. Kurai gave Shi-ria an annoyed look.

"I didn't know you were familiar with the Bible. Not being Christian myself, I'm not that familiar with it," Shinjo confessed.

"After meeting with the Order of the Cross, I was curious to understand their religion. But I digress." Shi-ria resumed her story, "Like many new religions, the Taman Knights were originally persecuted by the governments, established religions or people who simply didn't understand their powers and philosophies. In addition, the Taman religion promoted equality between genders, which went against many philosophies that traditionally were skewed in favour of males. This was the primary reason for creating the guards and training followers in self-defence. Many who followed these teaching were persecuted and forced to live in hiding. The Taman Knights fought many battles against invading armies. Countless wars greatly reduced their numbers. Due to constant warfare and battle, more and more Taman Knights began using the Koldar, drawing on negative emotions like anger, aggression, and hatred to give themselves strength. Divisions soon began forming in the Taman Knights as some began to feel that the only way to survive was to destroy the invaders before they were destroyed."

"A Taman knight called Turai-thol believed the only way to stop these constant attacks was by launching counter-attacks at the various hostile nations." Kurai added, "His growing aggressive behaviour began to cause concern among the knights. Some, like master Turai-thol, felt that using the Kolri to control the Koldar had been keeping the Taman Knights from exploring the full potential of their powers. He began to teach others that the Taman Knights were above right and wrong and justified in doing whatever it took to accomplish their goals. Proof of this came after he and a group of students were ambushed by pirates while visiting a town. After witnessing several of his students killed, Turai-thol murdered the pirates in a fit of rage. This was the main factor in the decision of the knights to expel him from the order. When he left, he took many other Taman Knights with him. These dark Taman Knights began forming their own code, a twisted perversion of the Taman code, one that stated that the Koldar was the source of true power and that the Kolri was not only unnecessary to control it, but it also held the Taman Knights back. They used their powers to subdue those who had persecuted them and rule over them. Since they relied solely on the inner darkness of the Koldar, they began to call themselves 'Koldar Warriors.' Eventually, this term came to refer to any dark Taman Knight."

Rirk took over the story again, "The Koldar Warriors soon began building their own empire by attacking many of the other nations of Thalia. Seeing the threat they now possessed, the Taman Knights formed a truce with many of the nations of Thalia to defend them from this growing threat. While some still didn't trust the Taman Knights, others began to realize that persecuting them was wrong. Ultimately, what proved to be the undoing of the Koldar Warriors was not outside forces but their own philosophies. Due to their anger, greed, and lust for power, many of them turned to infighting, and constant rivalries broke out as various Koldar Warriors tried to overthrow each other and seize power for themselves. This allowed the Taman Knights to defeat them since the Taman Knights could unite against their common enemy, while the Koldar Warriors were too busy fighting among themselves.

While the Taman Knights could defeat the Koldar Warriors, they realized that as long as the temptation of the Koldar existed, the Koldar Warriors would never truly be destroyed. Thus, the Taman Knights set up a strict code that hid all knowledge of the Koldar for fear that its power would tempt any Taman Knight who learned of this. They also took young children with an affinity for the Taman to train them. They justified that it was necessary for them to be taken while young so that they wouldn't develop emotional attachments to things, places, and people. They also forbade them from marrying or pursuing relationships as they believed such things would cause them to act selfishly and turn them to the Koldar."

"And that's how you three came to join the Taman Knights?" Shinjo asked.

"Not exactly," Rirk explained. "Hundreds of years later, a Taman Master named Kamatra began to question the teachings of the Taman Order publicly. He felt that forbidding knowledge of the Koldar didn't stop Taman Knights from being corrupted by it but made it more appealing. He felt it was better to teach Taman Knights about the Koldar to help them see its destructive power and help them resist its lure. He also felt that emotional attachment didn't necessarily lead to the Koldar, recounting how another Taman Knight who fell to the Koldar during the Second Koldar War secretly married and had a child prior to his fall. The Taman Council countered that this emotional attachment led to his fall, but Kamatra countered that had his relationship not been forbidden, he might not have turned to the Koldar. He also pointed out how this man's son, another Taman Knight, later saved his father due to the love they shared for each other. Despite this, the Taman council was still set in their ways. Kamatra felt the Taman Knights were stuck in the past and that their destruction was inevitable if they didn't learn to change and adapt to the times. His teachings were considered heresy, and he was expelled from the order. As a result, he relocated to this region of Thalia and started his own branch, our branch that Shi-ria, Kurai, and myself belong to—the Kamatra sect."

"Unlike the Alderoth sect, or the 'old believers' as we sometimes call them," Shi-ria chimed in, "our sect doesn't forbid emotional attachment, nor do we follow the one master/one apprentice model. Also, unlike the Alderoth sect, who believe only certain individuals can become Taman Knights, we believe that this power lies dormant in all of us. Thus, all beings can learn and use the Taman; thus, anyone can join as there are no age restrictions unlike the Alderoth sect."

"This power lies dormant in all of us?" Shinjo asked doubtfully. "So anyone can walk in off the street and say, 'I wanna be a Taman Knight' and *BOOM!* They become one?"

"Not exactly," Rirk laughed, "it takes skill, practice, and patience. Think of it as learning to sing. Some people are naturally gifted and can sing in perfect pitch; some even without any formal training. Yet others could spend their whole lives working hard at it and maybe learn to sing over time if they keep at it. And some will give it a try, only to give up because they don't have the patience to wait or they can't be bothered to put in the effort necessary."

"But that aside," Kurai said, resuming the story, "when word of our sect got around to the Alderoth sect, their grandmaster, Master Daisho, claimed our branch was composed of 'false' Taman Knights who had been corrupted by the Koldar. He claimed the members of our branch were Koldar Warriors who were deluding ourselves by following a 'false prophet.' Using his position as grand master and his influence on the government, he started the Taman Civil War in his mission to destroy our sect. Eventually, followers of the Alderoth sect and the government began to see that in his zeal to destroy us, he was slowly becoming the very thing he was trying to destroy. He was eventually stripped of his title and expelled from the order. Under direct orders from the government, our two branches were officially recognized and made peace through the Treaty of Jungsai. Despite both sects being officially recognized as legitimate branches of the Taman religion and officially being allies, there still remained some minor hostility due to their differing ideologies."

Shinjo shook his head, "This is a lot to take in."

"I know," Shi-ria soothed, "I'm sorry if it seems overwhelming."

LOCATION: BASE OF THE KOLDAR WARRIORS, PLANET THALIA

The base of the Koldar Warriors was old and run-down. It once belonged to an ancient cult that worshipped nature. Similar to the ancient tribe that taught princess Alderoth. What became of this tribe however, was lost to history. The Koldar Warriors didn't know and didn't care. As far as they were concerned, if this tribe no longer existed, it simply meant they were too weak to defend themselves and their home. This was the philosophy of the Koldar Warriors: the strong survive, the weak perish. This particular group of Koldar Warriors had originally been Taman Knights who willingly followed Master Daisho after he had been expelled from the

Alderoth branch. Like him, they foolishly believed themselves to be "true" Taman Knights. While Daisho's original mission had been to destroy the "false" Taman Knights, the Kamatra sect, they had allowed their self-righteous prejudice to expand until they saw all other religions as false and all other people as "infidels" to either be converted to their religion or to be destroyed. This was their new mission: to spread their teachings across the galaxy and to force everyone to convert to their religion, whether they wanted to or not. They wanted to build a galaxy-spanning theocratic empire.

This was how they ended up inadvertently playing a part in both Zolida and Knightwalker's game. They had learned about the same magic spell Zolida used to send Shi-ria to Earth, and they were planning to use it to spread their teachings across the galaxy. As far as the governments of Thalia and the other worlds of the Galactic Alliance were concerned, the Koldar Warriors were criminals and terrorists. If any of them were discovered on any alien worlds, the authorities would have them arrested on sight. While the Koldar Warriors' powers gave them an advantage over ordinary species, beings with a mystical force, such as mages, could hold their own against them. If they could gain access to the same magic Zolida used, they would be able to travel instantaneously to any world in the galaxy covertly. And once they were entrenched in said world, it would be very difficult for the authorities to have them removed.

In the original timeline that Scarlet Knightwalker came from, the cult found this spell five years ago. It was around the same time that Kurai had been taken. Having another Taman apprentice from the "false" Taman branch convert to their "true" religion was a pleasant bonus for them. When Shi-ria went to rescue her sister, the Koldar Warriors used Shi-ria as a test subject. They used the spell to send her off to a remote corner of the galaxy, not knowing where she'd end up and not really caring. They never knew she ended up on Earth, trained an apprentice of her own, only to die with Tokijin and Noonien. They never knew about the future that Knightwalker had come from. They never knew because Knightwalker had travelled back in time to prevent this incident from happening. Using the same concealment Zolida used at the police station, coupled with the potion Knightwalker used at the station, she convinced the Taman Knights to follow Shi-ria and rescue Kurai; thus, preventing this cult from sending Shi-ria to Earth. Knightwalker then used her magic to take the spell and destroy it so that it would never fall into their hands. No one knew that Scarlet Knightwalker had been there the whole time, making sure that history didn't repeat itself. The only one who knew the truth was Zolida. Thanks to Knightwalker, the future had been altered, so

Zolida was determined to make Knightwalker's job as difficult as possible.

Using her magic, Zolida teleported directly into the central chamber of the temple of the Koldar Warriors. Unlike Scarlet Knightwalker five years earlier, Zolida didn't bother to conceal herself; she wanted them to know of her arrival. Thus, the Koldar Warriors were genuinely surprised when this strange woman magically appeared before them. "An intruder!" one of the warriors shouted.

"Trespassing in our sacred halls is an act of sacrilege!" another called out.

The various other members all murmured in agreement. Using the same Taman alchemy that the Taman Knights possessed, they created various melee weapons. They moved toward Zolida, preparing to attack. Zolida simply waved her hand and lifted each of them up in the air and hurled them backwards with her magic. Some slammed into the walls, others into each other. Master Shodo, the current leader of this cult, was the only one not affected by this. He was a middle-aged man, though years of relying on the power of the Koldar began taking its toll on his body. His hair, what little of it he had left, was grey. His face was pale and pock-marked. His skin was saggy and wrinkled, and his purple eyes were bloodshot with dark circles surrounding them; he looked as though he hadn't slept for days. Despite this, he was still quite muscular, though it wasn't noticeable as he wore a bulky suit of metallic armour over a black silk dress shirt and baggy black trousers tucked into heavy black leather boots. He simply stood watching. Using the power of the Taman, he tried to read her, just as Shi-ria had when she first encountered her. All he sensed from her was her presence, nothing more.

Zolida turned to face him, "If your followers are finished making fools of themselves, perhaps we could talk."

Various Koldar Warriors slowly got to their feet, weapons at the ready, but Shodo, without taking his eyes off Zolida, simply raised his left hand. The Koldar Warriors stopped in their tracks. Obviously, Zolida's power had piqued his curiosity. So he was willing to hear what she had to say. "Who are you?" he demanded.

"My name is Zolida," she responded. "I'm a sorceress. Beyond that, who I am and where I'm from is of no importance to you."

"And what is it that you want?"

"The question isn't what *I* want," she corrected, "but what is it that *you* want? I know about your history, Master Shodo. How over a hundred years ago, Master Kamatra left the Alderoth branch of the Taman Knights and formed the Kamatra branch. How Master Daisho saw these heretics as traitors who distorted the teachings of the Taman Knights and how the rest of the fools on the Taman Council kowtowed to the Thalien government; too afraid to stand up to them."

"They were fools!" Shodo barked. "Cowards! Too spineless to see that Kamatra was a traitor and that his followers were perverting the teachings of the Taman Knights! Master Daisho knew this, but the rest of them couldn't see beyond their own selfish needs! The need to appease the government to remain in their good graces! 'Cause they were afraid of losing their favour with the government. A true Taman Knight wouldn't submit to the whims of the ignorant masses! He'd use his superior skills and intellect to make them see they're the ones who are wrong! That they are the ones who must be forced to submit to the enlightened!"

Zolida smiled subtly. It was just as she hoped. Like Knightwalker had done earlier at the police station, she used the same magic potion to make the Koldar Warriors more susceptible to her suggestion. Of course, there was the risk that, like Shi-ria, the Koldar Warriors might realize what was going on. Their Koldar senses might warn them something was off, but this was less likely to happen. Unlike the Taman Knights, these Koldar Warriors were ruled by their emotions, their passion, their aggression. This made them easier to manipulate. As long as Zolida told them what they wanted to hear, they'd be more inclined to do as she said. Strong emotions often tended to cloud one's better judgment. By appealing to their arrogant assumption that they were "true" Taman Knights, a lie that they had successfully fooled themselves into believing, by telling them what they wanted to hear, she could make them do whatever she wanted. All she had to do was make them believe it was their idea.

"Just as you do," Zolida soothed, appealing to his ego. "Unfortunately, when the enlightened are greatly outnumbered by the ignorant masses, it's hard to make them see the light. Which brings me to why I'm here. Do you remember how five years ago you were searching for an ancient spell—one that would allow you to instantly teleport anywhere in the galaxy without using the gateways and going through official channels at Orathos?"

Shodo nodded; he remembered the incident perfectly. Normally, beings were forced to use their planet's gateway to travel to the central hub on the planet Orathos. Without such gateways, the only way to travel from one planet to another was via a spaceship equipped with a means to travel faster than light. Since Shodo and his band of Koldar Warriors were labelled as terrorists, they were banned from leaving Thalia. Even if they had managed to gain access to Thalia's gateways, make it to Orathos, then travel to another world, the authorities would be alerted. Thus, they'd be forced to fight off hordes of Taman Knights or other mages who would try and stop them.

However, if they had the means to bypass the planetary gateways, they could sneak onto various alien worlds, spread their doctrine, recruit new followers, all the while conquering and subjugating other infidels. And by the time the Taman Knights—or other planetary governments—realized what was going on, they would already be too deeply entrenched to be removed. This was their plan. Shodo heard rumours about such an ancient spell—one thought to have been lost centuries ago. He had his minions searching Thalia for any relics that supposedly held clues as to how to find or perform this spell. It was five years ago that he had been close to finding it when one of his followers had tried to recruit a Taman apprentice named Kurai. However, it turned out to be an ambush by the Taman Knights; at least, he believed it to be one. Kurai's fellow apprentices, Shi-ria and Rirk, along with their master Kalai-Udon and the rest of the Kamatra sect, followed her and ambushed his followers. With their plans discovered, Shodo and his followers were forced to go into further hiding.

"You remember how the Kamatra sect found out about your group and stopped you? What you didn't realize was that a sorceress named Scarlet Knightwalker was behind it all," Zolida lied. The truth was that originally, Shodo and his cult found the spell when Shi-ria showed up to try and rescue Kurai. In the process, Shi-ria was sent to Earth. This was how events unfolded in the timeline Knightwalker originally came from. When Knightwalker later travelled back in time to alter history, she made sure to prevent the Koldar Warriors from finding the spell. She covertly made sure the rest of the Taman Knights followed Shi-ria to stop this cult and prevent Shi-ria from coming to Earth. Unaware of this, Shodo and his followers were forced to go back into hiding and continue their futile search. So, they continued searching caves and other ancient archaeological sites for any relics that could help them. One such site was a cave. The very cave Shi-ria had been assigned to guard three months ago. Shodo had hired Dead-Eye to search and steal any relics in said cave in the hopes that there might be something there he could use to bring him one step closer to this power. Unfortunately, none of the relics there were of any use to him. "Scarlet Knightwalker used this spell to send Dead-Eye and a Taman Knight named Shi-ria to a planet called Earth," Zolida continued lying. "With them out of the way, she took the ancient scrolls the spell was written on and hid them away to ensure no one would ever find them. Surely with your powers, you know this to be true."

Shodo reached out with the power of the Koldar to see if she was lying. Unfortunately, Zolida's magic, combined with the potion, allowed her to manipulate him easily. Using her magic, she allowed his retro-cognitive abilities to see the events unfold the way she wanted him to see, not what really happened. "So, this Scarlet Knightwalker is to blame for our failures at procuring this spell," Shodo incorrectly deduced.

"Indeed she is," Zolida said and continued spinning her elaborate web of lies. "What's more, she's from the future. Originally, you succeeded in obtaining this spell and spread your empire across the galaxy. She's travelled back in time to prevent this from happening."

"WHAT?" Shodo shouted, his anger building up inside him.

"You succeeded in your mission," Zolida continued, "until she came back in time, altered history, and undid all your successes. That's why I'm here. I've also come back in time; to try and stop her and try and set history right once again."

Shodo stood up and roared, "This Scarlet Knightwalker will pay for her actions!"

A faint but sinister smile crept up in the corners of Zolida's lips. "In the future, I am but one of your many followers," she continued weaving her misleading tales. "My magic, combined with your powers, can overpower her. Together we can set things right again!"

Shodo smiled at her. Despite his arrogant belief in his superiority, Zolida had successfully played him like a fool. "Bring me this Knightwalker and the spell, Ms. Zolida, and I shall not forget your loyalty when we conquer the galaxy."

"Yes, master," she said, bowing. "And I know exactly how to bring her to you . . ."

Location: Transport Heading to the Capital City of Thalia

Shinjo stared out the window of the transport. The rocky desert terrain surrounding the Kamatra sect's headquarters gave way to grassy plains and eventually lush green forests. The odd town or farm whizzed by as the transport raced toward the planetary capital. Being a police officer, he had a keen sense of observation. He sat there, taking it all in. To some extent, Thalia didn't seem all that different than Earth, that is, except when they passed through various cities and towns. Though Shinjo only got brief glimpses of these alien urban areas, he couldn't help but marvel at the advanced technology of the planet. It made him realize how far behind Earth truly was in the cosmic sense. Shi-ria, Rirk, Kurai, and Shinjo were all on the transport to the capital city of Thalia. Their plan was to take Shinjo to the gateway, transport him to Andropolis on the planet Orathos, and from there, use the central gateway to return to Earth. This was the way most beings travelled from one planet to another without using spaceships.

Otherwise, people would need a ship with the ability to travel faster than light. They were explaining this to Shinjo.

". . . and these gateways allow you to travel from one world to another instantly?" he asked.

"Yes, via the central gateways on the planet Orathos," Shi-ria explained. "All gateways travel through the central gateway in the city of Andropolis."

"They're the only way to travel from one planet to another instantly," Kurai added.

"I've never seen or even heard of such a thing." Shinjo was overwhelmed by all of this.

"Actually, there are smaller versions of such gateways on other worlds, including Earth," Shi-ria explained. "That's how beings on Earth can sometimes travel great distances across the planet. Like how the Order of the Cross does so."

"The Order of the Cross has access to such power?" Shinjo asked.

Shi-ria nodded and said, "Mystic explained it to me. It's how they're able to instantly respond to demonic threats across the planet. Their headquarters are in Europe, in the Holy Roman Empire. Yet they were in Oyashima, a country on the far side of Asia. If they were to travel by conventional means, it would take them hours to get from Vatican City to Teikoku City."

"I've never even known such things existed," Shinjo confessed.

"Most humans, who have no mystical force, wouldn't know where to look or how to access them," Shi-ria explained. "Besides, I doubt they'd believe it if they were told. One of the things I've observed about Earthlings is that they have a remarkable ability to dismiss the blatantly obvious, even when it's staring them right in the face."

"Like I did when you told me you were an alien?" Shinjo asked.

Shi-ria bowed sheepishly, "I'm sorry if I offended you."

Kurai shook her head and said, "You should learn to be less judgmental, Shi-ria."

"Like you're one to talk," Shi-ria retorted. "Besides, I'm simply making an observation. If you want to travel from our headquarters to the capital city yet take a transport to Kalshiya instead, am I being judgmental in saying you're going the wrong way? Or am I simply making an observation?"

Kurai was about to answer when she stopped mid-sentence and stood up. Rirk and Shi-ria did the same. "I sense it too!" Rirk exclaimed.

"As do I!"

"Sense what?" Shinjo asked. Shi-ria was about to explain that her Taman senses warned her of danger when suddenly, their transport was rocked by an explosion.

"Stay here!" Shi-ria told Shinjo. Using their Taman alchemy, she, Kurai, and Rirk conjured up their Taman weapons. Shi-ria had her sword, while Rirk had a long red bo staff, and Kurai held a pair of ornate, sharp, metallic tonfas. Before they could investigate, their enemies fell upon them. The door to their car was kicked open and a group of Koldar Warriors, all with their weapons drawn, rushed in to confront the three Taman Knights. Shi-ria, Rirk, and Kurai knew they were Koldar Warriors. They could sense the dark energy of the Koldar emanating from them. While they didn't specifically recognize the faces of their attackers, the three Taman Knights remembered the familiar feeling radiating off these terrorists. It was exactly the same as when they were apprentices years ago. Shi-ria and Kurai still recalled when Shi-ria and Kurai had a fight in which Kurai gave into her anger and nearly killed Shi-ria. Only the interventions of Master Kalai Udon and Mistress Kalai Utra kept Kurai from killing Shi-ria. It was shortly after that the Koldar Warriors tried to turn Kurai to their side. Had it not been for Shi-ria and Rirk going to save her, Kurai might be one of these Koldar Warriors right now.

The Koldar Warriors didn't speak; they simply lunged at the three Taman Knights. Using the Koldar, they charged Shi-ria, Rirk, and Kurai, hoping their anger would give them the strength to overpower them. By contrast, Shi-ria, Rirk, and

Kurai used the Kolri to remain calm and keep their minds clear. As the Koldar Warriors attacked, Shi-ria and Rirk used the No kudai chenmol, the *form of air*, as it is translated, to defend themselves. Kudai chenmol was the "air form" because, like moving air currents, practitioners of this form used acrobatics to dodge and evade their attacks. Thus, Shi-ria and Rirk continually used their weapons to block their attackers' weapons while jumping and spinning to avoid them, hoping that in doing so, their opponents would become more frustrated that their rage would eventually blind them and would allow Rirk and Shi-ria to land a blow and incapacitate them. The problem with this form was that they had little room to maneuver in the confines of the transport car. Plus, the constant moving around would eventually wear them out. Thus, the Koldar Warriors could theoretically keep sending wave after wave of soldiers to attack them until they were too tired to continue fighting.

By contrast, Kurai used the No chido chenmol, the *form of earth*. It was called this because practitioners, like solid rock, stood their ground facing their attackers head-on and then returning said attacks with the crushing strength of a boulder. Kurai favoured this form over Kudai chenmol. She tapped into her Koldar to give herself strength while tempering it with the Kolri to ensure that she didn't give in to aggression like the Koldar Warriors. She effortlessly blocked her opponents' attacks, then concentrated her inner darkness to make quick and powerful strikes against the Koldar Warriors. Upon doing so, she quickly used the Kolri to calm herself before turning her attention to her next attacker. In the confines of the transport car, this form proved to be more advantageous than Shi-ria and Rirk's form. She wasn't struggling to move around in a confined space. However, the disadvantage for her was that she needed to use her strength to ensure a stronger opponent didn't overpower her. There was also the concern that if she tapped too much into the dark energy of the Koldar, she could lose herself to it and become a slave to its evil grip like these Koldar Warriors had become.

The Koldar Warriors relied on the No dalsai chenmol, the *form of fire*. This form was a dangerous one, so dangerous that the Alderoth sect forbade its use. Dalsai chenmol sacrificed defence for a strong offence. Practitioners of this form, like a raging fire burning out of control, swept in, attacking relentlessly, hoping to either overpower their opponents or simply wear them down until they could finally deliver the killing blow. Tapping into the unrestrained dark power of the Koldar, they attacked with the speed and ferocity of a burning wildfire, destroying everything in their path until nothing was left. Despite this, the three Taman Knights stood their ground. While the Koldar Warriors grew more frustrated and angry with each attack, the Taman Knights remained calm and collected during the battle. This was the problem the Koldar Warriors faced. While the Koldar gave them power, it came at a cost. The more aggressive they got, the more they gave into anger and hatred, the more desperate, more irrational they got in battle. Some of them already fell into this trap. Giving into to white-hot burning rage, they lunged at the three Taman Knights without thinking. Thus, Shi-ria, Rirk, and Kurai managed to take advantage of their mistakes. One lunged his sai directly at Rirk's throat, only for Rirk to easily sidestep and use his bo staff to strike his opponent in the back of his head, knocking him down. Another Koldar Warrior swung his sword wildly at Shi-ria's head. She simply ducked and used her sword to strike his right leg before spinning behind him and kicking him into a nearby empty seat, his head slamming into the armrest. While Kurai fell into a repeating pattern where her attacker would go to strike, she'd block with one tonfa and then use the other to strike back, either in the head or stomach. Sometimes she'd switch it up and use her foot to deliver a strong kick into her attackers' gut or even their crotch.

While all this was going on, Shinjo stood back, marvelling at the battle happening in front of him. While Shi-ria and Rirk moved with the agility of Olympic gymnasts, Kurai stood firmly like a statue in front of him, protecting him from their attackers, instinctively reacting to each attack like a machine on autopilot. Shinjo couldn't help but admire their skills. As a police officer, he had been trained in combat, mostly to protect himself and others from common criminals. He knew how to disarm thieves and take down suspects, but he had never faced opponents with skills like the Koldar Warriors. Unlike the others, Shinjo didn't have a connection to the Taman. He recalled Shiria's words about how such power lay dormant in everyone. If that were true and it was indeed inside of him, he had no idea how to tap into it. Even if it were possible for him to do so, he doubted it would happen in the next few seconds, nor would he instantly gain enough skill to take on such attackers. Unfortunately for him, this was a weakness their opponents had no objections to exploiting. One Koldar Warrior charged directly at Kurai. Just as before, she stood her ground, preparing to meet his attack head-on. Instead of using the power of the Koldar to attack, he used its power to enhance his movements as he effortlessly jumped over her, landing behind her and directly in front of Shinjo. Kurai had been caught off guard by this. She had sensed his rage as he charged her. She simply assumed that, like many Koldar Warriors, he was blindly charging into battle without thinking. Instead, it seemed he used his anger to hide his true intentions to attack

Shi-ria's friend from Earth. He couldn't tune into the Taman and had no other mystical force either. This Koldar Warrior obviously figured that out. He knew that Shinjo was a liability to them. Kurai silently cursed herself for not anticipating this. With all the dark energy of the Koldar surrounding her, with her being forced to constantly defend both herself and Shinjo from the relentless barrage of attacks, it made it hard for the Kolri to guide her. It was like trying to see through a thick fog. Despite this, she could still sense imminent danger from the other Koldar Warriors. As much as she wanted to turn to face Shinjo's attacker, the Kolri kept warning her not to turn around since more Koldar Warriors were continuing their attack. Thus, Kurai was in a bind: either turn and protect Shinjo and have the others attack her from behind or continue facing her attackers and have a Koldar Warrior attack Shinjo.

"Shi-ria!" Kurai called out. She didn't need to say more. Shi-ria turned her head and saw everything. Behind Kurai was a Koldar Warrior facing off against Shinjo. He had a pair of sais pointing directly at the detective. Shinjo tried to reach for his gun, which had fortunately been transported along with the rest of him to this planet. Unfortunately, the Koldar Warrior sensed this, and with his lightning-quick reflexes, slashed at Shinjo's hand, forcing him to drop his gun, which landed harmlessly at his feet. Seeing he was in danger, Shi-ria punched her current opponent in the face before leaping over the seats and other warriors to get to Shinjo. The Koldar Warrior sensed this. Grabbing Shinjo's injured hand, he twisted it and moved behind Shinjo, using him to shield himself from Shi-ria. Shi-ria landed directly in front of the two men just as the Koldar Warrior—using his free hand—drew his sai, pointing it directly at Shinjo's throat.

"Drop your weapons and surrender, or he dies!" the Koldar Warrior growled.

Shi-ria stopped dead in her tracks. She could sense that he wasn't bluffing. It was obvious that the Koldar Warriors were after the Taman Knights. As far as they were concerned, Shinjo was expendable.

"DO IT! ALL OF YOU! NOW!"

The battle ceased. Both Rirk and Kurai turned to see this Koldar Warrior holding Shi-ria's Earth friend hostage. Even with their enhanced Taman reflexes, there was no way they could help Shinjo before the Koldar Warrior delivered the killing blow. With no other choice, the three Taman Knights dropped their weapons. They had lost.

"Restrain them!" he ordered his fellow Koldar Warriors. The other warriors grabbed Shi-ria, Rirk, and Kurai and restrained their arms behind their backs. Two other Koldar Warriors approached the one holding Shinjo. They took him and restrained him too.

The one who originally attacked Shinjo—no longer holding his captive—turned to open a nearby door, exiting the transport. "Come, we have what we came for."

"Where are you taking us?" Shinjo demanded.

"To meet our master," the Koldar Warrior replied.

10

LOCATION: BASE OF THE KOLDAR WARRIORS

Shi-ria, Shinjo, Rirk, and Kurai stood in the temple of the Koldar Warriors. Various Koldar Warriors surrounded them. The four of them were at a disadvantage. They were greatly outnumbered, plus the Koldar Warriors had all the powers they, as Taman Knights, had. The only difference was that the Koldar Warriors lacked the moral centre of the Taman Knights. While the Taman Knights used the Kolri to temper the Koldar—their negative emotions—with love and compassion to ensure such dark powers were used for constructive, not destructive purposes, the Koldar Warriors did not. For them, the Kolri were chains that held them back, keeping them from reaching their full potential.

Shodo looked at Shinjo. It was obvious he wasn't Thalien. He could sense this man was confused and afraid. He liked this; he liked the idea of being feared. He looked Shinjo over, "I don't know you," was all he said. He then turned his attention to Shi-ria, Rirk, and Kurai, ". . . but you three, I remember you well . . . Rirk, Shi-ria, and . . . Kurai. Isn't it? I never thought I'd see your faces again."

"Shi-ria, who is this man?" Shinjo asked.

"His name is Shodo," Shi-ria explained. "Rirk, Kurai, and I first encountered him years ago when we were still apprentices."

"He tried to recruit me into his cult," Kurai added.

"A pity you turned us down," he countered. "You could have been saved and joined the true religion of the Taman Knights. Instead, you let yourself be deceived by the Kamatra cult. You allowed yourself to be willingly taken in by their lies!"

"It is you that let yourself be deceived into thinking you are the true followers of the teachings of Alderoth," Kurai countered. "A Taman Knight would never behave the way you have."

Shodo simply shook his head, "You just don't understand; Master Daisho did. He knew that as long as there were unbelievers and heretics like your Master Kamatra, we would never be truly safe. They would try to destroy us, pervert our teachings! Thus, we have to destroy them to protect ourselves!"

"Destroy who?" Shinjo asked.

"Anyone who refuses to follow their teachings," Rirk answered.

"Anyone who refuses to follow our enlightened philosophy," Shodo corrected.

"Any person who forces their beliefs on others and threatens to kill those who refuse to follow is hardly what I would call 'enlightened,'" Shi-ria countered.

"You simply don't understand," a familiar female voice called out from the shadows. Both Shi-ria and Shinjo recognized it immediately. Zolida stepped out and stood next to Shodo.

Kurai turned to Shi-ria, "Is this Zolida?"

Shi-ria nodded.

"She has offered us something of great value," Shodo added.

"What?" Shi-ria asked.

"You," he grinned, staring directly at her.

"Me?"

"As a hostage," he added. "Zolida explained to us that you were transported instantaneously across the galaxy by a woman named Scarlet

Knightwalker. But that's impossible, now isn't it? Ordinarily, one uses the planetary gateway to travel to Orathos and then to whatever world they wish. But to be able to bypass that, to be able to go anywhere in the galaxy, any world, any part of that world . . ."

Shi-ria, Rirk, and Kurai gave each other uneasy looks. Shodo and the other Koldar Warriors could sense their concern. ". . . yes!" Shodo nodded. "With such power, we could once again spread our empire across the galaxy."

"Again?" Shi-ria asked, feigning ignorance. She feared Zolida told them how events had originally unfolded and how Scarlet Knightwalker went back in time to change things. Shi-ria was trying to figure out a way to get them out of their predicament, but she needed time. She hoped she could buy some by playing dumb.

"Come now, Shi-ria," Zolida interjected. "Don't you remember the last time you faced off against these people? They were trying to find an ancient spell—a spell lost to time—that would have enabled them to do as Scarlet did. They would have sent you to Earth back then had she not intervened and made sure they never found the spell." Suddenly, it all made sense to Shi-ria. Was that why Zolida brought Shi-ria to Earth three months ago? Was she trying to ensure that history repeated as it was originally supposed to?

"Once they have Knightwalker, they can use her magic to teleport anywhere they want in the galaxy," Zolida told them.

"We can spread our theocracy across the galaxy," Shodo grinned wickedly. "All will follow our will—the true teachings of the Taman Knights—and those who refuse to submit to us will be destroyed!" An uneasy feeling came over Shi-ria, Shinjo, Rirk, and Kurai. If the Koldar Warriors had such power at their disposal, it made them even more dangerous. They could teleport anywhere in the galaxy, to any place on any planet. They could recruit new followers, assassinate anyone who might be a potential threat, and disappear before anyone even realized what was going on. The three Taman Knights knew they couldn't allow this to happen. They had to stop them no matter what. The problem was they were greatly outnumbered. Even with Shinjo's help, there were dozens of Koldar Warriors. If only the four of them could escape, they could warn the Taman Council. Then all Shi-ria, Shinjo, Rirk, and Kurai would need to do is hide until help arrived. The problem was this wasn't just an ordinary band of thieves; these were Koldar Warriors. They had the same powers as the Taman Knights, nullifying any advantage the three Taman Knights would have. Fortunately, Shi-ria saw another advantage. It was obvious that Zolida had been misleading the Koldar Warriors. Thinking that her being sent to Earth was the work of Scarlet Knightwalker, Shi-ria knew that if the Koldar Warriors captured Scarlet Knightwalker, they would try to torture the information out of her. That was why Zolida made it look like Knightwalker was the one with the power. Shi-ria figured that Zolida wanted to ensure the Koldar Warriors didn't turn on her. Shi-ria found the advantage they needed.

"What do you need Scarlet Knightwalker for?" Shi-ria asked. "You already have what you need right here." She gestured toward Zolida.

An uneasy feeling came over Zolida.

"Didn't you know? It was her and not Scarlet Knightwalker who brought me to Earth," Shi-ria explained. The Koldar Warriors turned and looked at Zolida. While they still couldn't sense anything from her, the look on her face made her feelings clear. She didn't want Shi-ria telling them this.

"SHUT UP!" Zolida barked.

"On the contrary," Shodo countered, "I'd like to hear what she has to say." He turned to Shi-ria and said, "Continue!"

"As I said, Zolida was the one who used her magic to bring me to Earth. It was Scarlet Knightwalker who tried to stop her. Zolida was probably hoping you'd destroy her enemy, destroy Knightwalker for her, since she couldn't do it herself," Shi-ria explained. "Either that or after Knightwalker defeated all of you, she'd be too weak to fight; thus, Zolida could finish her off with little effort." Shi-ria paused as she smelled a familiar scent. She recognized it as the same one Knightwalker used back in the police station. "Furthermore, Zolida is manipulating you via a magic potion. I recognize that scent. Whoever smells it easily falls under her sway. No doubt she used it to make you less hostile and more willing to agree with her plan. I'm surprised your Koldar senses didn't detect it already," Shi-ria taunted the Koldar Warriors. "Perhaps relying solely on the Koldar and not the whole Taman doesn't make you stronger as you claim."

Now Zolida was in trouble. The magic potion she used was the same as the one Knightwalker used back at the police station. While it was usually quite effective, it did have one disadvantage. If the person under the spell's influence were to realize this, the spell would no longer work. In a way, the spell wasn't much different than what this cult was doing to its various members. Like any cult, it brainwashed followers into espousing their views while making them think they are their own. If the victim realizes they're being manipulated, they'll naturally resist. Like being in a cult, no one knows they're in a cult until they get out. "She's lying!" Zolida stammered.

"Am I?" Shi-ria turned to Shodo. "Use your Taman senses. They'll confirm that I'm telling the truth." Shodo reached out with the power of the

Koldar. Like the Taman Knights, the power didn't give him the ability to read their minds directly, but it confirmed Shi-ria wasn't trying to deceive him.

Shodo turned to Zolida, "So, you planned on using us as your tools? Because you were too weak, too scared to fight this Knightwalker person!"

"I'M STRONGER THAN SCARLET COULD EVER HOPE TO BECOME!" Zolida shouted. If there was one thing she couldn't stand it was taking a beating to her ego.

The Koldar Warriors turned their weapons on Zolida and surrounded her. "Then we have no need for this Knightwalker person," Shodo deduced. "You'll show us how to use this power!"

Zolida scowled at Shodo. She wasn't about to be bullied by this little cultist. "Or what, you'll kill me? With my magic, I'm more powerful than any of you could ever hope to be!" Zolida prepared to use her magic to fight off the Koldar Warriors only to find that something was preventing her from doing so. It didn't take her long to figure out what was going on. "Scarlet!" she shouted. "I know you're here somewhere! Show yourself!" No one responded. The Koldar Warriors all reached out with their Taman senses, as did Shi-ria, Rirk, and Kurai. However, none of them could sense anything. If Scarlet Knightwalker were here, she was using her magic to conceal herself from them.

Even with their Taman senses, none of them could sense her, not even her presence.

Seeing that the Koldar Warriors were focused on Zolida, Shi-ria looked over at Shinjo, Rirk, and Kurai. She didn't speak, but she didn't need to; one look was all they needed to know what she was planning. Using their Taman alchemy, the three Taman Knights began to break down their restraints, molecule by molecule. Then they used it to transform their restraints into their weapons. Shi-ria leaned over and whispered in Shinjo's ear, "The three of us will create a distraction. Run for the exit and don't stop. Get as far away as you can, then contact the Taman Council. Tell them everything that happened. Tell them to send help."

"What about you three?" he whispered. "You're greatly outnumbered. You can't fight them all off."

"Don't worry about that," Shi-ria reassured him. "We are luminous beings, temporarily housed in these physical bodies. They may destroy our bodies, but they can't destroy our souls."

"This isn't a philosophy class, Shi-ria. You . . ."

"We don't have time to argue, detective," Shi-ria explained. "Remember what we told you about our Taman alchemy? The Koldar Warriors have the same power. The difference is they have no objections to using such power on living beings. Imagine if one of them decided to use such power on *you*, detective."

Shinjo recalled the incident back in the park when that mugger pulled his knife on Shi-ria. He remembered watching it disintegrate right before his eyes. He didn't understand how Shi-ria did that until she explained Taman alchemy to him. Shinjo never realized that if they could do such things to inanimate objects, then what would stop them from doing so to a living person. Shinjo's stomach turned. He didn't like the idea of the molecules in his body, his cells, his internal organs being taken apart atom by atom. He also didn't like the idea of abandoning Shi-ria, Rirk, and Kurai, but he had to admit Shi-ria had a point. He assumed that the Taman Knights had some way of protecting themselves from falling victim to such an attack. Unfortunately, he wasn't so lucky. He turned to Shi-ria and nodded. Both turned their attention back to the Koldar Warriors, who, fortunately, seemed to have turned their aggression toward Zolida.

"She's right here, right now!" Zolida stammered. "Can't you sense it?"

"ENOUGH!" Shodo bellowed. "Your attempt to stall and distract us isn't working!" Shodo used the same Taman alchemy Shi-ria, Rirk, and Kurai had been using. But he didn't use it to conjure up a weapon. Instead, he focused it on Zolida, targeting the atoms in the very cells in her body and breaking them down one by one. Zolida began to feel pain deep inside her. She clutched her stomach and fell to her knees. "Show us how to use this power," Shodo ordered, "or I'll keep this up until you're dead!"

Shi-ria turned to Shinjo and nodded. He turned and ran for the exit.

"HEY, YOU!" one of the Koldar Warriors called out. The others turned to face their captives. Before they could stop him, the three Taman Knights were upon them. Kurai used her Chido chenmol—earth form—to strike two warriors in their guts with her tonfas. While Shi-ria and Rirk, relying on their Kudai chenmol—air form—to attack as well. Shi-ria leapt in the air, kicking several opponents in their faces before landing and delivering more spinning kicks before using her sword to block their attacks. Then with the speed, agility, and grace of a gymnast, she spun and dodged further attacks. Meanwhile, Rirk used his bo staff to jab his opponents in their guts, then, raising his stick, struck them in their faces. Like Shi-ria, he twisted and turned, dodging attacks while simultaneously using the high end of his bo staff to block and deflect his opponents' weapons while using the lower end to swoop at their feet and knock them to the floor.

The commotion caused Shodo to stop his attack on Zolida and turn his focus back to the Taman Knights. Taking advantage of this, Zolida, ignoring the pain in her abdomen, turned and ran out of the chambers down a hallway. She didn't know where she was going; all she hoped for was to get away alive. Unfortunately for her, Shodo sensed this.

"Stop her!" he barked at two of his followers. "Bring her back alive!"

"Yes, master." They both bowed and took off after her.

Shodo turned back to his hostages. Seeing his minions attacking the Taman Knights, he figured they could handle them, so he focused on the fourth hostage, the one who wasn't a Taman Knight. Knowing he was a liability to them in battle, he figured the three knights were trying to buy him time to escape. Shodo knew that if Shinjo escaped, he'd try to warn the other Taman Knights, and Shodo couldn't let that happen.

***

Zolida ran down the hallways, away from the chamber where the battle was taking place, running as far as she could from the Koldar Warriors. Because of the blocking spell Knightwalker had cast on her, she had no way to use her magic, and without her magic, she was at a disadvantage. She turned right down one corridor, then left down another, then left again, then right. She had no idea where she was going; she prayed that she'd find a way to escape, hopefully, while her pursuers were running around in circles trying to find her.

She only wished she wouldn't accidentally run into them. As she turned another corner, she stopped suddenly. There, standing directly in her path, was Scarlet Knightwalker.

"This was all part of your plan, wasn't it?" Knightwalker deduced. "Have me try to rescue them so that the Koldar Warriors find out about me, forcing me to stop them, or worse, kill them!"

A sinister grin came across Zolida's face, and she said, "You were so concerned about Shi-ria not coming to Earth, not training her apprentice. So, I just figured I'd do you a favour."

"Don't give me that!" Knightwalker scowled. "You and I both know that the Koldar Warriors would have killed her along with the rest of them."

"If Shi-ria's dead, then you don't have to worry about history repeating itself, Scarlet," Zolida taunted. "Unless, of course, you don't want Shi-ria's death on your conscience." Zolida was right. As much as Scarlet Knightwalker didn't want Shi-ria on Earth, as much as she didn't want her to find and train her future apprentice and risk having history unfold as it did before, Knightwalker drew the line at killing an innocent woman. Even if Knightwalker didn't actually commit murder, as far as she was concerned, knowingly leaving Shi-ria to die made her just as guilty as the person actually doing the killing. This was one major difference between the two. While Knightwalker was more than capable of taking a life, she would never consider such an option. On the other hand, Zolida had no objections to using others as tools to achieve her goals and had no problem with them being disposed of when she was done with them. Knightwalker knew this as well; that's when she got an idea. She decided to give Zolida a taste of her own medicine. Knightwalker used her magic to cast a blocking spell on Zolida earlier. With this spell in place, it didn't matter what kind of magic Zolida tried to use; the blocking spell automatically nullified any of Zolida's magic. For the moment, Zolida was an ordinary, magicless human, just like Knightwalker. The only difference was that Knightwalker still had her magic staves. Grabbing one of them, she focused her thoughts, and the staff reacted, firing out a wispy black tendril of magic energy. It grabbed Zolida and restrained her. "What are you doing?" Zolida demanded.

"This is part of *my plan*," Knightwalker taunted Zolida, throwing her own words right back at her. "Now they know about you and can use you and your powers to teleport anywhere across the galaxy. Now let's see if *you'll* stop them! I'm betting you're not willing to sacrifice your life for their cause!"

Knightwalker was right. While Zolida had no qualms about letting others die, she had no intention of sacrificing herself. But she had another idea. "The question is, are *you* willing to let me die, Scarlet?" Zolida taunted. "I know you won't take a life!"

"I won't be the one killing you," Knightwalker countered.

"But you'll be leaving me here to die," Zolida continued. "Meaning my blood will still be on your hands!" Zolida words smacked Scarlet Knightwalker harder than any punch. As much as she loathed to admit it, Zolida was right. Before she had been found by Zolida and their late master, Scarlet Knightwalker had been a bounty hunter. However, unlike most bounty hunters, she had a strong sense of morals. She never accepted jobs from disreputable clients, nor did she act as a mercenary for hire. It was her job to capture dangerous criminals and bring them to justice, not decide justice for herself, nor carry out sentences. Knightwalker hoped that the threat of being killed would have compelled Zolida to surrender. Instead, Zolida was gambling that Knightwalker wouldn't let her die. Knightwalker knew that the Koldar Warriors would have no objections to killing anyone.

Just then, the two Koldar Warriors sent to recapture Zolida arrived. They stopped dead in their tracks upon seeing Scarlet Knightwalker.

"Who are you?" one of them demanded.

"Who do you think she is?" Zolida snarled.

Knightwalker turned to face them but said nothing.

"So, you're this Scarlet Knightwalker, are you?" the other Koldar Warrior deduced. They drew their weapons. "You'll come with us now!" Again, Knightwalker didn't answer; she simply reached behind and grabbed one of her many staves. "Oh no, you don't!" the Koldar Warrior shouted. He and his partner drew their weapons and lunged at her. Ordinarily, a person without a mystical force would be at a disadvantage against two Koldar Warriors, but her magic staff helped to level the playing field. Holding the staff in her hands, she let it guide her movements and actions. It told her when to block their attacks and when and where to move to dodge their attacks. It also allowed her to overcome the strain of having to twist and contort her body in such a rapid sequence of movements. Having been crippled a long time ago trying to save innocent lives, Knightwalker had been left for dead, only to be discovered by Zolida and their late master. Having taken her back to their pocket dimension, she spent the next several decades learning to move and fight again, thanks to magic healing spells. Without them, she undoubtedly would have remained completely paralyzed from the neck down. But even with this advantage, her staves couldn't sustain her forever. It was only a matter of time before pain starting creeping back throughout her body and before her injuries would slowly start to hinder her combat skills. Eventually, she'd twist, turn or contort her body in a matter that would cause her to suddenly spasm in pain. That was if one of her opponents didn't get lucky and land a blow on her. However, Knightwalker had another idea. Using her magic, she released Zolida from her magic restraints.

Zolida didn't understand why Knightwalker released her, but she's wasn't about to throw away such an advantage. "Thanks, fool!" And with that, Zolida took off.

"Stop!" one of the Koldar Warriors shouted as he turned to chase after Zolida.

"Forget her," the other one told him. "We need to capture Scarlet Knightwalker and bring her back to the master." They turned back only to find themselves staring down an empty corridor. The Koldar Warriors only turned their attention away from Knightwalker for a few seconds, but during that time, she managed to escape and do so without leaving any trace of where she went.

"SHE'S GONE!" the first Koldar Warrior shouted.

"I CAN SEE THAT, FOOL!" the other chastised him.

"How is that possible?"

"Her magic!" the second Koldar Warrior deduced. Their Koldar abilities would have typically sensed someone trying to escape, but thanks to Knightwalker's magic staves, they granted her abilities beyond an ordinary human. The Koldar Warriors knew they were in trouble.

If Shodo found out what happened, they'd both be blamed for letting both Zolida and Knightwalker escape and probably be killed for failure. Their only hope was to try and find Zolida. Because of Knightwalker's magic staves, they couldn't sense her at all. But Zolida's magic was still being temporarily blocked by Knightwalker's blocking spell. Hopefully, they could find her before she escaped, or the spell wore off, in which case, Zolida would have her magic back and would easily be a match for both of them. Filling their minds with feelings of rage, thoughts of what tortures they'd unleash upon Zolida when they'd find her, they surrendered themselves to the dark energies of the Koldar, letting it guide them to their target—Zolida.

***

Back in the main hall, Shi-ria, Rirk, and Kurai continued fighting off the Koldar Warriors. Unlike on the train, Shi-ria and Rirk had plenty of room to maneuver. Allowing the Taman to guide them, Rirk and Shi-ria used their Kudai chenmol to dodge their opponents' attacks. It also allowed them to remain calm while the Koldar Warriors, drawing on their rage, grew increasingly frustrated, trying to land a blow on their evasive opponents. Unfortunately, while their anger gave them strength, it cost them their strategy. The Koldar Warriors' frustration caused them to simply charge at them like a bunch of wild animals. This allowed both Shi-ria and Rirk to strike and take them down easily.

"This is almost too easy," Shi-ria remarked.

Kurai rolled her eyes. Using her Chido chenmol, she stood firmly like a boulder, blocking her opponents' attacks and striking back with the crushing force of a massive boulder. "I see you're still not taking combat seriously. I would have thought that after all these years, you'd learn not to underestimate your opponents."

"And *I* would have thought that after all these years, *you'd* learn to lighten up and not be the grouchy stick-in-the-mud you always used to be," Shi-ria taunted.

"I'm not a stick-in-the-mud!" Kurai retorted. "Just ask Rirk; he'll tell you that I can be fun and jovial!"

"He's your husband now," Shi-ria teased. "It doesn't matter what you say; he has to respond with 'yes dear.' Isn't that right?" she said, turning to Rirk.

"It would be best if you two remembered that the Koldar Warriors are our enemies at the moment!" Rirk scolded them. "Focus your attacks on *them!* Once we're all safely back home, then you two can fight the way you always do."

"We're not fighting!" Shi-ria countered. "We're . . ." she stopped mid-sentence. She sensed something was wrong. She turned around to see Shodo standing behind Shinjo; his blade was at Shinjo's neck.

"Drop your weapons, or he dies!" Shodo ordered.

The battle stopped. The Three Taman Knights dropped their weapons on the floor.

"Now," Shodo spoke, "Since Zolida can perform this spell, I no longer need any of you to contact this Scarlet Knightwalker." He turned to his followers and said, "Kill them all." The Koldar Warriors raised their weapons, preparing to finish their hostages off once and for all. Suddenly, they all sensed the presence of more intruders with the same spiritual powers as them.

Shodo and the Koldar Warriors turned around. There, standing behind them in the doorway that Shinjo attempted to escape from just a few minutes ago, were even more Taman Knights of the Kamatra sect. There were dozens upon dozens of them, and they all had their weapons drawn. Master Kalai-Udon approached Shodo.

"Master Kalai-Udon," Shodo recognized him instantly. "One of the leaders of this false branch of Taman Knights."

Kalai-Udon raised his eyebrow as he gazed into Shodo's eyes, "You accuse the Kamatra sect of being a 'false branch of Taman Knights' when you and your followers delude yourselves into thinking *you* are still Taman Knights. A *true*

Taman Knight has no desire to force his beliefs upon others. A true Taman Knight would not have such an obsessive zeal for destroying those who do not share their beliefs. And a true Taman Knight would certainly *never* threaten to kill an innocent man."

"All who do not share our views are infidels!" Shodo countered. "They would seek to destroy us, so we must either convert them or destroy them!"

Master Kalai-Udon shook his head. "If you truly believe that, then you have learned nothing from the teachings of the book of Taman."

The various Koldar Warriors shouted in rage. They considered it a great insult for a "false Taman Knight" to make such an accusation against their leader. While they were more than willing and eager to engage the Taman Knights in battle, Shodo knew better. If Shodo and his followers were to start fighting all the Taman Knights right here and now, the odds were that most of them would end up dead. However, if they were to surrender, they would survive. The Taman Knights were known for their compassion. While the Taman Knights were capable of killing, they would only do so if left with no other option. There was also the matter of the government of Thalia. Hundreds of years ago, when Master Kamatra first formed his branch of the Taman Knights, Master Daisho lead the followers of Alderoth on a quest to destroy them. The government of

Thalia was forced to intervene. Under the terms of the treaty of Jungsai, the government formally recognized both branches of the Taman Knights as legitimate. While the government of Thalia would most likely dismiss Shodo's cult as a terrorist organization, they wouldn't approve of the Taman Knights taking the law into their own hands and simply killing all of them. Thus, if Shodo and his followers chose to surrender, the Taman Knights would be legally bound to take them in alive. Shodo and his followers simply had to bide their time until they could escape and start the process all over again. Such compassion was a weakness of a democratic republic like Thalia. A weakness that, for the moment, Shodo and his followers could exploit. Thus, Shodo released his hostage and dropped his weapon.

"Stand down," he ordered his followers.

The other Koldar Warriors shouted in protest.

"NOW!" Shodo barked.

Reluctantly, the other Koldar Warriors dropped their weapons and surrendered, some still grumbling about not getting to fight to the death.

Master Kalai-Udon turned to his three former apprentices and Shinjo and said, "Are you all right?"

"Yes, master." The three of them bowed respectfully.

"Impeccable timing, master," Shi-ria added.

"We came as soon as we got your message," Kalai-Udon explained.

Shi-ria, Rirk, and Kurai all stared at him in confusion.

"What message, master?" Kurai asked.

Kalai-Udon stared at them with confusion. "You did not send a message telling us you were under attack by these Koldar Warriors?"

The three of them shook their heads.

"We were ambushed, then captured," Rirk explained. "We never had a chance to send a distress signal."

"How odd . . ." Mistress Kalai-Utra pondered. "We received a text message telling us to come here because you four had been ambushed by this cult of Koldar Warriors. We assumed it was you who sent the message asking for help."

"I assure you that none of us sent any message," Shi-ria explained. However, she wondered whether Scarlet Knightwalker was the one who did so.

Location: A Public Park, Teikoku City

With Shodo and his cult safely incarcerated for the moment, Shi-ria was able to take Shinjo to the capital of Thalia, through the gateway to Andropolis, and then back to Earth. After saying goodbye to her family, she and Shinjo found themselves back on Earth. Soon they were back in Teikoku City.

Shinjo turned to Shi-ria, "Well, Ms. Shi-ria, that was . . . quite an adventure."

Shi-ria bowed politely. "I apologize for all the trouble we may have caused you, detective."

Shinjo smiled and said, "It's all right. It's not every day that a police officer gets to travel to an alien world in another part of the galaxy. Though I'm not sure how I'm going to explain all of this to my superiors."

"Why not simply tell them the truth?" Shi-ria suggested.

Shinjo chuckled at the thought. "You really think they'd believe me?"

Shi-ria couldn't help but laugh herself. "Probably not," she admitted. "What about me, then? Are you going to take me into custody?"

"You and your siblings helped save my life," Shinjo replied. "I can't exactly arrest you for that, now can I?"

"So, what will you tell your superiors then?"

Shinjo shrugged. "You and your 'cousin' managed to get away from me. I spent all that time trying to find you with no luck. My superior won't be happy, but this will just end up being another one of those cases that hasn't been solved yet."

"If that's what you feel is best, detective." Shi-ria bowed once again. "Good luck, Detective Shinjo."

Shinjo bowed politely in return, then turned and walked off. Shi-ria was now standing alone in the park. But she wasn't alone for long; she felt a familiar presence approach, one she recognized from before.

"It was you who alerted the Taman Knights to our predicament, wasn't it?" Shi-ria called out.

"I did," a familiar female voice replied from the shadows. Shi-ria turned around to see Scarlet Knightwalker emerge.

"Now that the detective is back home, do you intend to send me back to Thalia?" Shi-ria asked.

Knightwalker thought it over, then said, "What was it you said earlier about the 'law of attraction'?"

"You mean how I said that the more your thoughts focus on trying to prevent the future you don't want, the more you make it happen?"

Knightwalker nodded. "As you pointed out, I've already altered history. Thus, who knows what will happen now."

"So, you've decided to let me stay? At least until I complete my mission and capture Dead-Eye?" Shi-ria asked.

Knightwalker nodded.

"And what of this apprentice I'm supposed to meet and train?"

Knightwalker hesitated, then said, "We shall see."

Shi-ria raised her eyebrow with curiosity. "What made you change your mind?"

"You did," Knightwalker explained. "I've been watching you covertly for many years now, Ms. Shi-ria. You're obviously not the rash, impulsive person you once were. Perhaps now you can train your apprentice and make sure she doesn't fall into the same trap she did in *my* past."

"I have faith in the Taman," Shi-ria explained. "It has never let me down." And with that, Shi-ria bowed politely before turning to leave.

Knightwalker bowed as Shi-ria walked away. *Let's hope for all our sakes that your faith is not misplaced, Ms. Shi-ria,* she thought.

*The adventure continues in
Mystical Force, Volume 4 . . .*

CPSIA information can be obtained
at www.ICGtesting.com
Printed in the USA
LVHW090354211021
701042LV00001B/67